# Master *of*
# Disguise

*Hidden Truths Vol. 6*

# Master *of* Disguise

## Wendy VanHatten

DocUmeant *Publishing*
244 5th Avenue
Suite G-200
NY, NY 10001
646-233-4366
*www.DocUmeantPublishing.com*

# Master of Disguise

*Hidden Truths Series, Vol. 6*

Published by DocUmeant Publishing 244 5th Avenue, Suite G-200 NY, NY 10001

Phone: 646-233-4366

Copy Editor JoAnn Rasmussen

Cover Design and Layout Ginger Marks
DocUmeantDesigns.com

Printed in The United States of America

ISBN13: 978-1-9378-0180-9 (14.99 USD)

# Dedication

This book is dedicated to my husband, Rick, who encourages me to write. Of course, Shadow, my office kitty, assists in my work.

# $\mathcal{O}$ne

**SAMI KNEW MEN.**

She was good at interpreting what they wanted from her, and how to read them. After all, she had been posing for men and their cameras since her early teen years, and their cameras loved her. Her dynamite smile, her fresh look, her professionalism . . . all of it. For her, it was more than a job. It was her passion.

But, this man scared her.

He wanted something; something he had been ranting about for the past hour. She was certain she knew exactly what he wanted, and that was a problem for her. She didn't have them.

When he glared at her, it felt like he could see right through her. She had seen that look one other time, and it wasn't one she ever wanted to see again. But, here she was. How on earth could she have misread him? For that matter, how was she going to get out of here? She was in the middle of the Pacific Ocean, for Pete's sake. When he spoke again, she jerked her attention back to the man.

"For the last time, where are they?" Sitting across the table from her in the galley of his yacht, he was completely the opposite of when she met him at the party the day before. His sweet smile had disappeared; his warm caresses gone. This was a man focused on getting what he wanted.

Sami licked her lips, lowered her eyelids, and cautiously looked around. She had never been on a boat this large, nor one with an upper and a lower deck, and she had been impressed at first. Impressed with the gleaming brass handrails, dazzling chandeliers above the table, cozy sitting area, and smooth ride. She took note of everything, including the wine he served, the delicate crystal glasses, the elaborate spread of sharp cheeses, spicy salami, and salty olives, and the bites of melt-in-your-mouth dark chocolate. She had also been impressed with the man himself. Until now.

His large hands, each wearing a gleaming ring, were tightly fisted as he clenched them on the table in front of Sami. Those hands reminded her of paws she had seen on a lion during a photo shoot on safari; huge and powerful.

Her fear was growing, the muscles in her stomach tightening. "I already told you. I don't have them. Besides, they were a gift from a friend." She tried to sound brave.

"Oh yeah? Who?"

"My boyfriend gave them to me." Sami shrugged her shoulders and lowered her eyes. "They were too gaudy, so I gave them back to him. I don't like to wear things like that." She hoped her lie would come out sounding like she meant what she said.

Quicker than she could look up, he grabbed her hands and squeezed, engulfing her small hands in his strong grasp.

"Ow, you're hurting me! Why do you care where that bracelet and earrings are anyway? They're probably just fake."

He squeezed tighter. "Why don't you be a good girl, and tell me your boyfriend's name. I'll buy them from him, and you can get something you like. Okay?" His thumb stroked her wrist, his gaze bore into her eyes. This was not a friendly request.

Sami struggled to free her hands, but his grip was too tight. "His name is Peter Smith. At least that's his business name. He's a photographer for some big magazines. I'm a model, you know. A famous one." She smiled her signature smile, hoping he would let go of her hands.

"Oh, so he's duped you, too? Let me tell you about so-called Peter Smith. First, he's not a real photographer and second, that's only one name he goes by. He's a jewel thief and those were stolen items he gave to you. Now, let's be civil about this. Where is he, and where is the jewelry?" He stood up, pulling Sami to her feet, never letting go of her. Her deep green eyes widened as his six foot three, well- built frame towered above her five foot, nine-inch, model-thin one.

Her eyes widened as she shook her head, her long red hair floating around her face. "I swear I didn't know they were stolen. I don't know where he is or how to find him. We only get together when . . ." She didn't see him move or have time to react as he let go of her hands and backhanded her across her cheek. Her head snapped back, shock registered on her face, and tears filled her eyes. One fist grabbed her hair, causing her to wince in pain as tears fell on her quickly swelling cheek. The other fist pounded the table, threatening to knock over the half-empty, crystal wine glasses as the olives bounced and rolled off the marble cheese board.

"I'm done playing games. Where are they?" His face was so close to hers, she could see the little red lines in his eyes, feel his breath on her forehead. She struggled to stay upright as he yanked her hair back. Panic set in, and she tried to kick him. Her eyes darted back and forth across his face and around the cabin.

Then, as abruptly as he grabbed her, he let her go, and she sank back onto the cushioned seat. "That's only a small taste of what will happen if you don't tell me what I want to know. Got it?"

She nodded, as she wiped tears from her face with her hand, flinching at the pain. Calmly, he took a sip of wine, set the glass down, and leaned across the table. "I really don't want to hurt you. I just want what is mine. Understand?" He looked Sami in the face. "Your friend, Peter, or whatever name he goes by, stole several items from me. That bracelet and those earrings were a small part of what he took. If I find him, I can get all my jewelry back. Then, the two of you can go merrily on your way. Okay?

"Now, just tell me how to find him. I'll take you back to Sausalito, but, if I were you, I'd ditch Peter. He's bad news." Again, he smiled at Sami. She thought he looked a lot like that lion who just found his latest meal. She shuddered and looked down.

That's when she saw the small knife, which had also slid off the cheese board when he hit the table. It was lying on the cushion right next to her. Casually, she reached down and palmed it as she tossed her hair back and stared at him. "I am so sorry, but I really have no idea where he is. I can send him a text." She slid her phone out of her purse with her other hand.

This seemed to enrage him more as he grabbed her phone and flung it against the wall. He stood up, towering over her as she tried to disappear into the cushion. "For the last time, tell me where they are. There is no way I believe you gave them back. No woman would do that." He started to reach for her again, but she moved sideways away from him. Then, she turned and lunged at him with the knife. It wasn't large, but it was sharp. Blood erupted from the nasty gash on his forearm. They both stared at the wound, as his pristine white shirt turned bright red from the sputtering blood.

He reacted first. Grabbing Sami with his uninjured arm, he swung her around, and held her up against him. Kicking and punching, she tried to free herself. Blood was dripping onto the floor, making it hard to get any traction in her four-inch stilettos. Just as she broke free, he picked up the knife, managed to get ahold of her hair, brought her closer, and stabbed her in the throat. More blood erupted onto the table and the floor. Sami went down, unmoving.

He picked up a towel, wrapped it tightly around his arm, and sat down. As soon as the light-headedness subsided, he bent down and rolled Sami over onto her back. Her lifeless eyes stared back at him. "Damn."

# Two

STILL A LITTLE unsteady, he stood up, found the first aid kit, and attempted to bandage his wound. Although the bleeding had slowed, it was still seeping through the gauze. He taped more gauze to it, then found another hand towel, and taped it around his arm. Satisfied he stopped the flow of blood, he started to clean up the mess. Everything bloody went into a large paper bag. Everything either he or Sami had touched, including his bloody shirt, followed. "Good thing I had on a different shirt when I rented this. I'm going to need it."

He found her purse on the table and her phone lying on the floor where he had flung it. Briefly looking in her purse, he found nothing of interest, and tossed it into the bag. He stuck her phone in his pocket. "Guess she really didn't have my jewelry. That means he does. I need to get this mess cleaned up, leave the boat, and find him."

He carried the bag up to the top deck, then went back down to drag Sami up. First, he had to find a towel to wipe up all the blood. Then, another one to wrap her in. With only one good arm, he had to stop several times before he managed to get her to the deck.

Finally, he cleaned up the blood from the lower floor, took the towels back up to the top, and tossed everything in the now-full paper bag. Positive he left no evidence of the struggle or the demise of Sami, he lit the paper bag on fire. When it had burned a little, he tossed it into the ocean and watched it float away, the flames dying as it sunk into the dark water. Then, he dragged Sami in the wrapped towel towards the edge of the deck and pushed her over the edge and into the ocean as well.

Her body floated as it slowly moved away from the boat. "Hope she sinks. Bitch." He looked out at the Pacific Ocean, past the Golden Gate Bridge, and saw no other boats. Turning back to the deck, he decided he had everything cleaned up, pulled up the anchor, and headed back to Sausalito. He wasn't worried about the boat rental place identifying him as he had put his wig, cap, and glasses back on. That disguise, the fact he rented it under a false name, and his overly-pronounced accent made him confident no one would be the wiser.

He'd look at her phone when he got home. He needed to find Peter, or Petrov, or whatever his current name was, and retrieve his jewelry. He knew exactly which pieces he had taken from him and needed them back. His buyers were waiting. One client wanted the largest diamond bracelet, and he was impatient. Not to mention ruthless. That worried him. But, then he remembered his favorite piece. The ring. His ring. It alone was worth everything to him. It would take a special buyer for that one, when he decided to sell it. He had to find it. Sooner than later.

These were no ordinary pieces of jewelry, after all. These old diamonds were worth multiple millions, at least, on the black market. He had spent months devising the plan to steal them from the old broad in Paris and a good week getting them out of her mansion. It was just bad luck he needed to involve anyone else in that heist. He should have known better than to let Petrov live after he was finished with him. He really was bad news. The thought of him with his jewelry continued to gnaw at him.

Time to find that scoundrel, get his jewelry back, and get rid of him. Maybe Sami really didn't know where he was, but her phone might be able to help him.

# Three

**THE WIND WAS** cold, but that was nothing new. Marta expected that as she played with her new camera and lenses, taking photos of the ocean, sailboats, cargo ships, the surfers, seal rocks below her, and even trying to get shots of the Golden Gate Bridge. She wanted good shots, but she also wanted to learn all the settings, what they did, and which ones worked best for her.

As a travel consultant and trip organizer, good photos were necessary to entice those who wanted to hire her for travel advice or to sign up for one of her special tours. It had been a year since her photos of San Francisco were updated, and now she had a new camera. She was having fun experimenting. Her best shots would go to her marketing guru in hopes he could use some of them.

She thought she had several good shots of sailboats and cargo ships, especially with the clear blue skies, and deep blue water setting off the gleaming white sails. Waiting patiently for a cruise ship sailing under the Golden Gate, she managed to take a picture-postcard shot. "Sweet." The Golden Gate Bridge photos always attracted attention.

Looking at her phone, she figured her fiancé, Clark, would be arriving soon to meet her for a late lunch. She always got excited when thinking of him that way. "I am so lucky." Deciding she had time for a couple more shots, she scanned the area for something she might have missed. One boat caught her eye as she adjusted the high-powered telephoto lens, and zoomed in on the large boat. "It's really a beauty. I know I'd want a big boat if I was going to be out there. The water's rough, currents are strong, and the captain had better know where the channel is."

As she took several shots, it dawned on her there was some-one on board tossing things into the ocean. "Damn. That makes me mad. Don't those idiots realize, you don't just toss your garbage into the ocean. Some poor fish or dolphins will get sick, or worse. I wish I could see them better and call the Coast Guard. They deserve to be given a citation."

She finished taking shots after the yacht moved away from her view and toward the bridge. Still frustrated, she walked into the restaurant and to their table. She must have looked upset as the lady at the next table asked her if she was okay.

"Yeah. I'm fine. I was trying out my new camera and lens and caught some dude tossing his garbage into the ocean."

"I hate that, too. You didn't get his boat number, did you?"

"I don't think so. He was kind of far away. We'll just have to hope the garbage doesn't do any damage." Marta put her camera away. "But, thanks for asking. I'm Marta Swenson, by the way."

"Nice to meet you. I'm Karla O'Rourke." She dug in her purse and handed a card to Marta. "If you did manage to get his boat number, I could turn it in for you."

Marta looked at her card. "Detective O'Rourke, thanks. But, I don't really think I got anything that would help. It just makes me mad." Marta shook her head as she sat down. "We probably know some of the same people. My fiancé is a private investigator and independent contractor for different agencies. I'm in the travel business." Marta handed her own business card to Karla.

"Really. What's his name? I might even know him."

"Here he comes now." Marta stood up as Clark arrived at the table and kissed her. "Clark, meet Detective Karla O'Rourke from the SFPD. Karla, Clark Moreno."

Talking for a few minutes, they realized they had several con-tacts in common, including Karla's boss, who was at Quantico with

Clark. "Small world, huh? Tell George I need to stop in and see him anyway about a new case. I'll let him fill you in."

Clark turned to Marta and smiled. Karla thanked him, then looked at her phone.

After several more minutes, Karla picked up her purse and turned to Marta and Clark. "Well, it looks like my sister is a no-show again. She may have been called for a shoot or she may have just spaced me off. Who knows? But, I gotta get back to work. Nice to meet you both."

# $\mathcal{F}$our

"I'M SO GLAD you're back. It seemed like you were gone forever. Maybe we need another vacation. But, I suppose I can wait until our honeymoon." Marta smiled at Clark. "So, can you tell me anything about Paris? It was jewelry, right?"

"I miss you, too, and I like the sound of another vacation. We could squeeze one in after your Venice trip and before our honeymoon, couldn't we?" Clark leaned over and kissed Marta again as she smiled.

"But, unfortunately, business first. Yes, I can tell you about some of the case as it's public knowledge. You're right. I went to Paris to investigate a jewelry theft. At the time, I wondered why Interpol wanted me involved in stolen jewelry, especially if it was a Paris issue. It turns out it was a little more complicated than that. An extremely wealthy lady had quite the collection of jewelry, mostly diamonds. Some of these could be traced back in history and all were quite spectacular individually. Put them together as a collection, and they were unbelievable. They were worth millions, at least. Some for their brilliance and quality alone; some for their historical value."

"Whoa. What does someone do with that many diamonds? I mean, do you actually wear them?"

"I really do believe she wore most of them. And, some had been in her family for centuries. So, their value was truly sentimental."

"Yeah, right. Millions of dollars of sentiment!"

"Right. Anyway, her collection was stolen. All of it. Poof. Gone."

"That had to be a ton of jewelry. What happened? Why Interpol?"

"Long story, and some of it is still being pieced together. This lady, and I can't yet tell you her name, and her family had this spectacular collection. Some pieces are reported to have intriguing history, including gambling, swindling, and murder, but I don't have those details yet. For all we know, those could be fantastic rumors passed down through the years.

"Anyway, she would often loan pieces for special events, fundraisers, and such. There were always guards accompanying the pieces and they never had any trouble. This lady was unmarried, with only one nephew left in the family. Since she was getting up there in age, the nephew and she were working with attorneys, museums, and foundations to divide up the collection.

"She kept the jewelry in a large safe in a special room at her mansion. Alarms were everywhere; the grounds, the mansion, the room the safe was in, the safe. You name it, there was an alarm. At least once a year a hush-hush drill was held with the Paris police. Response time was quick, so no one was worried about a break-in or a robbery." Clark took a bite of lunch and a drink of wine which had arrived while he was talking.

"But, something must have happened. You said they were stolen."

"This is where we're still putting everything together. About three months ago, the lady had a small stroke and the nephew came to live with her. She was doing okay, according to her physicians, but still had some trouble remembering certain things. She was adamant about not going to a nursing home or recovery facility. She wanted to stay at home.

"So, the nephew agreed to come live with her until she recovered completely. He was an investment broker, so it worked out well. This arrangement was going along smoothly, until she missed two doctor appointments.

"When those doctor offices called her and then called the nephew to check out why she missed the appointments . . . neither one answered. One office became concerned enough to call the police. They had to break in to her mansion and guess what they found?"

"I'm not getting a warm, fuzzy feeling about this. What happened?"

"They found the lady, dead in her living room."

"Oh no. How did she die? What about the nephew?"

"She died of blunt force trauma to her head, according to the medical examiner."

"How terrible. Did the nephew do it?"

"Well, he was the first suspect they thought of. But, later that same day, he turned up along the river bank. Shot through the head."

"What? What's going on?"

Clark's phone rang and he looked at the screen. "Sorry, but I do need to take this call. I'll be right back."

"I understand."

He excused himself.

# $\mathcal{F}$ive

MARTA WAS LOOKING at her camera and scrolling through the photos she took when he returned.

"Sorry about that. You know Ian, from Interpol. He wanted to give me a little more information. This entire case just gets more confusing by the hour. By the way, he says to tell you hello and he's glad things have calmed down a little for us after the fiascoes and issues you had in Venice. I think he views you as an unofficial part of the team by now."

"Sweet. He's a great guy and I feel like I've known him forever. So, what else is going on?"

"Okay. I told you the nephew turned up dead. The body was in pretty bad shape and the M.E. just got back to Ian with a time of death of approximately a week to 10 days ago. With decomposition and everything, he can't be exact. But, it was prior to the lady's death, which has now been narrowed down to four days prior to the doctor's office calling."

"I'm confused. Wouldn't he be missed at work, by the aunt, or somebody?"

"His work schedule was basically on his own time and he didn't have to report in to anybody, so no one noticed he wasn't around. Besides, his colleagues knew he was caring for his aunt. So, no red flags there.

"Like I mentioned, the doctor's office is the one who called the police to report his aunt not showing up for an appointment. But, that was just a timing issue.

"But, this is where it gets even more confusing. Ian and the investigation team found a couple of security cameras in her mansion. One is near the front door and one in the hallway by the room where the safe is. We briefly looked at them before I left to come here. That was before we knew about the nephew."

"And?"

"The nephew is seen coming and going at the front door." Clark paused.

"Okay. That's not unusual, right? I mean you did say he lived there now."

"Right. Except, he's seen coming in after she was killed."

"Oh no. So, the nephew did kill her. No. Wait a minute. Is the M.E. sure he died earlier than her?"

"Positive."

"Then, how and why was he coming into the house after he was dead?"

"Now you're thinking like part of the investigative team. Ian's agents are reviewing the camera footage again, frame by frame. They already discovered one issue, and that's another reason he called. Previously, when the nephew came to the mansion he would always look toward the camera. Even if he didn't directly look at it, he seemed to be checking it.

"For a day prior to, and for at least one day after the M.E. puts her death, the nephew is avoiding the camera. His head is down, his collar is pulled up, he has a large hat on. It's like he completely changed the way he enters the mansion. They're enhancing the footage now, and Ian will get back to me."

"Okay. But, I'm still confused on why Interpol is involved."

"I can tell you that part later. For right now, Ian is working on issues and informed me I might have to make a quick trip to Paris, and then come back here to finish the rest of the case."

"What's the rest of the case?"

"Ian wants me to be undercover as a buyer of diamonds. Apparently, I'm rich beyond belief, and I want old diamonds.

I don't care how much I have to pay, I don't care where they came from, and I'm ruthless. Want to be my rich girlfriend?"

"When do we start? Do I get to go to Paris?"

# Six

AFTER ONE MORE final check, making sure everything was clean, and there was no evidence of Sami or her death, he returned the yacht to the marina in Sausalito. The sleepy-eyed agent took his paperwork, stamped it complete, and nodded good-bye to him. He was more interested in a group of lovely young ladies who were looking at renting paddleboards than he was in his old-guy yacht renter.

"Okay, time to head to the condo, check out her phone, and rewrap my arm. Then, I've got to find that scumbag and get my jewelry back. I need those diamonds before anyone realizes they're missing, and I gotta have that ring." Navigating his rented luxury car through tourist traffic and onto the Golden Gate Bridge, he made it to his rented condo in just under an hour.

Once inside, he tried to access Sami's phone. "Damn. I was hoping she wasn't smart enough to have a password. This isn't going to do me any good. Okay. What do I know about the situation? I know she was his girlfriend, but what else? Why were they at the party? They must live together because she mentioned him giving her the diamonds. She's a model. Maybe she's famous. I need to look at magazine sites and maybe I'll find her."

He pulled up fashion magazines on his computer and scrolled through them for a model named Sami, Sammy, or Sammie. After just a few minutes, he found one with her photo. "Bingo. That's her. Now, to find out more about her."

His internet search discovered she was a model, but not always a high-end fashion model. Reading her Facebook and Twitter pages led to several other, older sites where she had posed; not always fully clothed. "Hmm. Miss Sami had quite the past, it appears. I need to use that to find out where she lived and who she hung out with." After several more minutes, he was no closer to finding her address or her recent personal information.

His phone rang and he noticed it was from a private number. "This could be good or very bad." Punching the talk button, he answered. After a short conversation, in which he said very few words, he hung up. Sweating and shuddering, he tossed his phone across the room. "Damn. He's here. Why the hell is he in San Francisco? I don't like this development at all."

He looked around his condo, half expecting to see the man on the phone materialize in front of him. "He sounded like he knows where I live. This isn't good. He's getting more demanding by the day. That bracelet alone is worth at least a million to this buyer. And, he's not somebody I can put off. I already told him I had it, and he's anxious.

"Time to get to work finding Petrov. And, my diamonds. He's got them. I know he does. And, I need them. Now."

# $\mathcal{S}$even

**AFTER LUNCH, MARTA** and Clark headed home. Home was a stunning, completely remodeled, three story, Victorian-style home in the Pacific Heights area of San Francisco. When Marta's grandma left her a sizeable estate several years ago, she purchased this house, where she and Clark now live. Prior to moving in, Marta had first added a large, yet, functional chef's kitchen, with everything she needed for entertaining. Clark put his touches on the home with state-of-the-art security and two hidden safes. Stylish furniture, comfortable features, and her grandmother's antiques all blended well throughout the entire home.

Marta's first-floor office showcased photos from her trips around the world, as well as two special paintings from her grandma. Behind one of the paintings was one of the hidden wall safes. Clark had insisted on installing another smaller safe in the kitchen pantry, where she kept a few of the jewels left to her by her grandma. Her family had been part of the ruling family in Venice over a hundred years ago, and her grandma left all the family jewels to Marta. Much of it was on loan to various museums in Venice, but she kept a few, favorite pieces to wear for special occasions.

Marta's desk was the one her grandma used, and she remembered her sitting and writing new recipes for her pastry business.

Now, when Marta sat and worked there, she liked to think Grandma was always with her. After all, her grandma had raised her, as her parents were killed in a plane crash when she was younger. They had been each other's only family.

Next to one window in her office sat a perch for her big, fluffy Maine Coon cat, Shadow. He could be found there watching birds outside in the bushes and flowers most mornings, or napping in the sun.

They had turned the den into an office for Clark when they got engaged and he moved in. Comfy chairs faced his desk, and another painting hung on one wall. When Shadow wasn't watching birds, he was curled up on the cozy blankets in one of the chairs.

Soft, dark gray carpet in the inviting living room complimented the lighter gray plank floors in the kitchen and their offices.

Two separate patios, each facing a different direction, offered spectacular sunsets, early morning fog, or Alcatraz and the hills beyond. Depending upon the time of day, those were the perfect places to start your day with a cup of coffee or end your day with a glass of wine.

Four bedrooms and four baths comprised the second floor. As with the rest of their home, comfort and style blended in perfect harmony.

But, what Marta fell in love with was the third floor, with its fantastic windows, providing views of the City, the hills, and the Golden Gate Bridge. She was tempted to turn the entire floor into her office, yet she knew she'd never get any work done there. Instead, it became their private retreat.

Now, as they came into the house, Shadow, greeted her with a meow and then purred at Clark as he entered. Clark was on the phone, but bent down to pet him as he brought in his suitcase.

Ending his call and putting his phone in his pocket, he turned to Shadow. "Did you miss me, big guy?" Shadowed meowed and purred louder as Clark ran his hand along his back.

"Crazy cat. I'm gone for an hour, and you'd think I had been gone for months. Obviously, he was attention starved while you were in Paris."

"Right. I know you don't feed him or give him treats or attention. Clearly cat abuse." Clark chuckled and then stood up.

"That was Ian again. I don't need to go to Paris, as he put together a task force here. We meet in an hour regarding the heist and what he wants to happen on this end. He'll Skype in with us. Apparently, it is now a top priority. And, he'll explain the Interpol connection to all of us, as well as why we're meeting here.

"He has some FBI guys, some detectives from SFPD, and me. Not sure who else. I'll have to fill you in after I get home. We'll probably have another meeting later, and I'll get clearance for you to be there.

"Ian also has some more critical information about the nephew. I'll find out about that then as well. For now, I have to get to the meeting. I'll see you in a while. Let's go out to dinner tonight."

"I'd rather cook and stay in. We haven't caught up on everything yet. I need to check out my photos and see what I did right and where I could improve. I'll have wine and food when you get home."

"Sounds fantastic." Clark kissed Marta and gave Shadow a quick pet. "See you later."

# $\mathcal{E}$ight

WHILE CLARK WAS gone, Marta settled in to view her photos on her computer. "Wow, Shadow, I didn't realize I took so many." She organized them into folders, so she could figure out what she liked and where she needed to work on her settings. Over an hour later, she had deleted some and understood why they were no good. There were a few that were fantastic, and she put those into a folder for possible use on her website or brochures.

When she came to ones of the yacht, she again marveled at its size. Then, she saw the ones where the person dumped his garbage into the ocean. Once again, it upset her. "Damn it, Shadow. Why do people do that? I wonder if I can make this any sharper or if I can get the number on the side of the yacht."

She played with different settings, trying to enhance the number, but it was still unreadable to her. She did get a fairly good view of the man, though. "Maybe I could give these to the Coast Guard and they could find him. It would be worth a shot."

She put those in a separate folder, thinking she would show them to Clark.

When Clark returned home she had dinner almost ready. "Well, how did your meeting go? Anything you can tell me?"

"Lots of stuff. Let's have a glass of wine out on the terrace, and I'll start way back at the beginning. Ian likes the viewpoint you bring to the table, and gave me the okay to bring you up to speed, as you will now be an important part of this operation. You'll be my girlfriend when I try to buy some diamonds. By the way, Detective Karla O'Rourke is one of the detectives involved. I'll fill you in on her as well." They moved to the terrace, Clark took a sip of wine, and sighed. "Great wine.

"Okay. The old lady, whose name was Matilda, owned all the jewelry. Her collection was not a secret. In fact, quite the opposite. All of Paris, and probably gem or diamond aficionados from all over the world knew about it. That, plus her security, made it quite safe. Before her stroke, her nephew had taken more of an active role in her life, helping her finalize the foundation for children she had set up. He had moved in and had been living with her for at least six months before all this happened.

"Keep in mind she was still a little confused after her stroke. According to her physicians, she had been in perfect health prior to that, so this was something they were keeping an eye on. There were some short-term memory issues, and she had trouble with her eyesight, but she was improving slowly."

Marta nodded as Clark continued.

"Now, this is where it gets interesting. And, where the Paris police and Interpol think things went awry. Since the M.E. puts the nephew's time of death at least four days prior, they reviewed the front door camera footage carefully. It just isn't possible for the nephew to come and go if he's dead. Therefore, someone else is coming and going, pretending to be the nephew. With enhancing everything and projecting size, etc., the person is about the same size and build as the nephew.

"The nephew was six foot three inches tall, fairly normal build, with dark blonde hair cut short. The person coming into the mansion after the nephew's death is approximately six three or taller, broad shouldered and muscular, and wears a hat all the time. The nephew never wore a hat, or at least not in any footage they have. They can't see any hair on the second person, though. So, those are noticeable differences. There are no fingerprints, either, as he was wearing gloves. One thing that does stick out is the size of his hands. They appear to be rather large, even taking into consideration the fact that he's wearing gloves and the angle of the camera. Ian is going to check with the M.E. to see if the nephew also had large hands."

"Didn't you mention there was a security camera inside the house, by the room with the safe?"

"There was. However, it had been disabled. The last footage from it was about the time of the nephew's death. It's like it just quit working. Same thing with some of the alarms, but not all."

"How convenient."

"Right. Add up all these things, and it points to a person posing as the nephew. Since Matilda probably didn't see very well, and the size and shape were approximately the same as her nephew, she wouldn't have had any reason to be suspicious."

"But, wouldn't this imposter talk to her?"

"Possibly. Maybe she couldn't hear very well. Or, maybe the imposter wasn't there long enough for her to wonder about his voice. Who knows?"

# $\mathcal{N}$ine

"OKAY. SO, I'M guessing you and Ian believe the imposter took the diamonds. Right?"

"This is Ian's theory. This imposter somehow knew specifics about the diamonds, and knew when the nephew would be out of the house. Probably watching him come and go or even arranging a meeting away from the mansion. Then, he, or someone he hired, killed the nephew. The Paris police and Interpol are still working on exactly where he was killed. Then, the imposter made his way into the mansion, killed Matilda, and took the diamonds.

"Ian admits there are some holes in this theory. For instance, how did he know about the jewelry in the first place? I mean, all of Paris knew about it, but they didn't know it was in her mansion or that it was accessible. How did he know he could just waltz in and take it? How come he just happens to be about the same size as the nephew? Was that premeditated? How come Matilda didn't recognize something was wrong, if the nephew had been gone for several days? Or, was she killed right after the nephew? Why didn't the alarms work? How did he get the diamonds out of the mansion? Why are they here in San Francisco?" Clark took another drink of wine.

Marta nodded. "Here? Are you sure they're here? Are those the ones you'll be buying?"

"Yeah, pretty sure on all counts. In fact, that's the main reason Interpol is involved. Long story.

"First, last weekend, there was a huge, fancy, who's who type of party here in a mansion on Nob Hill. This is where Interpol first caught sight of something, as the owner has a state-of-the-art security system inside and out. Anyway, one of the security guys who was at the party is actually an SFPD detective, and was just filling in for his cousin who was sick. He recognized a man at the party as a thief from a bust they did here a few years ago and decided to keep an eye on him. He could only think of one reason this guy would be at a party where all the guests were decked out in their finest jewels, and it wasn't good.

"He also noticed the thief came to the party with a young lady, who was quite beautiful, so he was watching both of them. That's when he noticed a spectacular bracelet the young lady was wearing, and wondered if the thief had stolen it for his date. He was pretty sure the thief couldn't afford it. Keep in mind this bracelet was distinct enough to be recognized as something special. So, he kept watching, and guess what he discovered?"

"The thief tried to steal something from the party?"

"Close. He found his mark, an older lady with several diamond, bangle-type bracelets on each arm. This thief brings her champagne, sits down by her, and flirts with her. Then, he brings her some food and more champagne, all the while talking and smiling close to her face. After several minutes, he stands up and tells her he'll be right back. What she doesn't see right away is one of her bracelets is missing. The detective watches the whole scene, without the thief knowing it, and calls it in.

"Right after that, the thief leaves the party unnoticed, the young lady with him."

"Wow. He must be good."

"Exactly. Which was why the cop was watching him."

"But, how does that relate to Paris and that theft?"

"If that thief hadn't been at the party and hadn't stolen a bracelet from a lady, and if the security guard wasn't an SFPD detective who knew the thief, and if he hadn't noticed a fantastic bracelet on the thief's date, there would have been no reason for

SFPD to look at the footage from the party. But, it all happened, and they did look at the tape. That's when the bracelet on the young lady became more of an object of interest. Looking deeper, they discovered the bulletin about the stolen jewelry in Paris, saw a photo of a bracelet which looked exactly like the one at the party, and Ian was called. It was all a chain of events that just happened to fit, thanks to the sharp eyes of the detective at the party.

"Now, Ian has put a plan in place involving me as the buyer."

"Okay. But, that small time thief can't be the one who stole millions of dollars of diamonds, can he?"

"Who knows? Maybe. Or, maybe he's a partner of the thief. Maybe it's luck and he was in the right place at the right time, and ended up with a fortune. That's a piece of the puzzle we're missing."

"Right. But, how come you're buying the diamonds now? Doesn't it seem a little quick for you, Mister Ruthless Diamond Buyer, to know these are available? I mean, weren't they stolen only a week or so ago?"

"You are correct. However, here's what has happened. As you know, Ian has informants all over. One of those has been posing as a buyer of stolen goods, especially diamonds, for several years. This informant was contacted by a man he knows as Mr. J, before the Paris jewels were confirmed stolen. Before. The informant was told there would be some one-of-a-kind, fantastic diamonds and jewelry available and was asked to put out the word to the right people with the right money. Lots and lots of money.

"That alone is curious. The thief is a smug bastard. It's like he knew exactly when he'd have them. Like he had a plan in place for quite some time. So, this is where I come in. Ian arranged for me to be that informant's client. And, I'm going to buy some diamonds. With any luck, these are the Paris diamonds.

"Now the second piece. This Mr. J contacted another buyer. It's somebody Interpol has been watching for quite some time from China. This guy is multi-billion-dollar wealthy. But, he's not a nice person. Ruthless, callous, and cruel are words Ian used. The reason Ian is sure he was contacted by Mr. J, is that he's here in San Francisco as of yesterday. Something's up.

"The thief may or may not be Mr. J. But, he's involved somehow. What we do know is that he or whomever he works for is greedy, maybe this time too greedy. He sets his prices high, uses nothing he thinks can be traced, and makes his deals in secret places. Also, he doesn't hesitate to get rid of those he doesn't like or those he thinks crossed him. At least, that's the info from the informant."

"Are you, are we, in danger by wanting to buy these?"

"Possibly. You know there's always a danger."

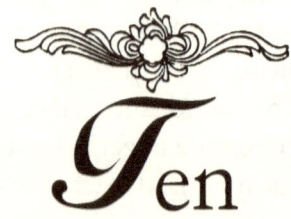

# Ten

**THE FOLLOWING DAY,** the man known as Mr. J
made a list of magazines, other photographers, and media people
in the Bay area. Then, he started calling. His real name, Gustav
Janssen, was known to few. His actual appearance was known
to even fewer than that. Speaking four languages, sometimes he
disguised his voice. Today, he used a French accent, but spoke
English.

He had to find Petrov, and he hoped information about Sami
would lead him to the scumbag. And his jewelry. After three calls,
he got lucky. A lady at this agency directed him to another one,
where she knew Sami was working. He sighed in relief as he placed
the next call.

"Yes, Mr. J, we have worked with a freelance photographer
by the name of Peter Smith. He's been great with one of our best
models, and is fantastic at getting that seductive smile out of Sami
time after time. I know they had a thing going for a while, but
Sami was so much better than him, if you ask me. Not that I would
tell tales or anything. But, you can tell these things after working in
the business for so long." The receptionist actually gushed on the
other end of the call. "At first, they were soooo cute together. But,
thank goodness she finally wised up, and that little arrangement is
changing. I do know for a fact . . ."

Interrupting her long-winded dialogue, he came across a little harsh. "Okay. I get it. They were an item. That's not why I'm calling." When he heard a gasp from her, he softened his tone. "Sorry. I've just had a hard time catching up with the pair. We used to hang out together, and I was in town for a convention. I wanted to see both of them before I leave town. I don't suppose you know where I could find them? Please. I mean, you sound like you really know things. You probably run the whole business, don't you?" He attempted to schmooze her, in hopes she would give him worthwhile information.

Knowing she really shouldn't give out personal information, the receptionist decided this time it wouldn't hurt. She was pretty sure Sami wasn't home, anyway. And, the apartment building had good security. "Well. I suppose. Sami has an apartment in my building, and I think Peter still crashes with her most of the time. Like I said, they were quite the couple for a while. I think things are cooling off, though. When you see them, tell Peter we have his check here. And, Sami is due for a shoot the end of this week. May I tell them you called and asked about them?"

"Sure. Tell them Mr. J called. I'm hoping to surprise them, but it will be okay. Thank you so much. You've been such a great help." He discontinued the call before she could respond.

Armed with an address, he went to work online checking out the security at the apartment building. He knew Sami wasn't there. But, he didn't know if Petrov was waiting for her or not. "Even if he's not there, I might find out something to lead me to him. I could get lucky and find my jewelry." In a matter of minutes, he found out companies and businesses who regularly delivered items to residents in the building, he found the name of the security company, and more. "This is too easy."

With that, he developed his plan and went to work on his disguise, name badge, and credentials. "Tomorrow at lunch time. By then, I'll have everything I need." He unlocked the outfitted, extra room in his condo, punched in a series of numbers on his designed safe-like case, and pulled out trays of gleaming, shimmering, mind-blowing jewelry. Once he had the room set up, he went to work removing some of the diamonds from their settings.

"Damn. I need that bracelet before my buyer realizes I don't have it. And, I really need that ring. It's mine." His eyes narrowed.

# Eleven

**PRECISELY AT NOON** the following day, Gustav walked up to the security guard at the apartment building where Sami lived. His uniform, badge, credentials, and demeanor portrayed someone who knew what he was doing and was used to getting his own way. Since he had already placed a call directly to the guard that morning telling him of a mandatory inspection by a fire chief, the guard chatted only for a couple of minutes as he glanced at the credentials. Gustav had his opportunity, and his plan was in place.

"Do you need me to do anything? Do I need to tell the residents anything?" The guard motioned toward the elevator door.

"Nope. Just do your job, and I'll do mine. You know these rules and regs are important, but people can get in the way. It will be a whole lot easier and quicker for you if I can get in and out without a lot of questions from folks. I should be done in about an hour. If I need you, I'll come back here."

The guard nodded as Gustav walked to the elevator, keeping his hat low on his face, but not worrying about anyone recognizing him. With his face, hair, and eyes heavily and creatively disguised, he was confident of that.

Once inside the elevator, Gustav went to the top floor. He figured the guard wouldn't think anything about him starting at the top and working his way down. The floor he wanted was the fifth one. Once he arrived at the eighth one, he switched elevators and went back down to five, arriving at the door to Sami's apartment.

Slipping on latex gloves, he listened carefully for noise. Out of the corner of his eye, he noticed a woman come out of a door at the other end of the hallway. She looked toward him, which concerned him briefly. But, then she walked to the elevator, stepped in, and left. Looking back at this door, he knocked. He waited. No noise at all. He pulled the small handgun with its silencer out of his pocket, and tried the door knob. As expected, it didn't budge. Pulling the pick out of another pocket, he carefully and silently picked the lock, and opened the door with his foot.

Unseen by him, the woman stepped back out of the elevator and watched him. "Curious. But, I don't have time to wonder about a fireman. I didn't hear any alarms, and I have to get back to work. I'll mention him to Ivan." She re-entered the elevator and pressed the ground floor button. Since Ivan was not at his desk by the front door, she left and promptly forgot about the fireman.

As he opened the door to her apartment, Gustav had the element of surprise.

"Sami, where the hell have you been? I've looked . . ." The man on the inside rushed toward the opening door, but didn't have a chance to finish his sentence. Once inside the apartment, Gustav shut the door, put his hand on the man's chest and shoved him through the small foyer toward the sofa. He pointed his weapon directly at him.

Even though he had a gun pointed at him, the man did a double take as he recognized Gustav. He smiled. "Hey. Am I glad to see . . ."

Gustav took two steps toward him and smacked him with his gun, causing him to wince as he fell backward onto the sofa. He tried to slide out of Gustav's way.

"You thought you could escape me. Well, you're wrong. Get up. We're going to have a little chat."

Looking up at Gustav, he gingerly slid to the edge of the sofa. "Man, don't shoot me. I just want . . ."

"Shut up. I'll do the talking." Gustav waved the handgun toward him. "Peter Smith. Is that the name you're going by now? You didn't think anyone would connect the name Petrov Smit to you, huh? Well, never mind. I don't care about your name. I want what you stole from me. Where are they?"

Holding up his hand, Peter looked at Gustav. "Don't shoot. Okay?" He swallowed.

"Tell me where they are, and we're good." He smiled, trying to put him at ease for the time being.

"Okay. Bear with me. And, don't shoot. I let my girlfriend wear them to a party, and she lost them."

"I know about the party. I was there and even talked to your girlfriend before you disappeared. But, what the hell were you thinking, letting her wear them? I have a buyer for those. Now, what do you mean she lost them?"

"What? You were at that party? I didn't see you."

"Never mind the party. Where are the earrings and bracelets? What'd you do with the ring?"

Petrov sighed, looked down at his hands, and took a deep breath. "She had them on when we left the party. I swear it. We made one stop so I could drop something with a friend."

"Yeah. I saw you take that diamond bangle right off the old broad's arm. She didn't even miss it. Now, what happened? Tell me everything, and I mean everything."

"Well, I knew I had a buyer for that bangle, so we stopped at this guy's place. I left Sami in the car. I couldn't have been gone more than 10 minutes or so. She was still sitting in the car when I got back. I was happy about the price I got for the bangle, so we stopped to celebrate. Had a bottle of champagne at a little bar we go to around the corner from here. Parked in the underground ramp."

"How long have you known her? What did you tell her? Where did she think you got the jewelry? Better question . . . why the hell did you steal them from me. Did you think I wouldn't find out?" Gustav waved his handgun toward Petrov's face.

He ducked. "Okay. Okay. We met about six months ago when I was helping out at a photo shoot. She thinks I'm a big time photographer who makes tons of money. Please don't tell her I'm not. I moved in here with her when I got back from Paris. She thinks I travel for work. I was expecting her back by now. I'm really worried about her."

"Back to what happened. You parked the car and went to the bar. Then, what?"

"We came back, went to bed, and woke up the next morning."

"What did she do with the jewelry?"

"I swear I saw her take off the bracelet and put it in her jewelry box that night. I figured it was okay for the night, and I'd take it out the next morning. She said she just got an invitation to go to a party on a boat, and she was excited. She mentioned meeting some guy at the party who wanted to talk to her about something. Anyway, I went to the coffee shop on the corner to get our morning coffee. She was ready to go when I got back, we had coffee, and she left.

"After a while I went to her jewelry box." He sighed. "It was empty. Only a few pieces were there. But, not the earrings and not the two bracelets and not the ring. She hadn't worn the ring at all. But, they were all gone." Petrov looked up. "I was going to give them back to you. I swear. I just wanted to impress her. That's why I took them." He gasped as Gustav pointed the gun at his head. "Don't shoot. I'll get them. I promise."

Gustav lowered the weapon. "Go on. And, please enlighten me on how you plan to return them when you already told me they were lost."

Hesitantly, he continued. "After Sami left, I went through the entire apartment. I couldn't find them anywhere. I texted her, asking where they were. That's when she told me she lost them. I knew that was a lie, because I saw her take off the bracelet and put it in her jewelry box. I'm sure she took everything off and put them in there. I know she didn't have them on when she left to go to the party. So, I texted and asked when and where she lost them." He sighed again and put his head in his hands. "I never heard back from her. And, now she's gone. Do you think she sold them and disappeared?"

# Twelve

GUSTAV HAD A dilemma on his hands. It wasn't that he minded getting rid of Petrov. That was going to happen anyway, once the job was finished. But, Petrov had become an immediate liability and he certainly didn't need him around any longer. What he needed was the diamonds. All of them. And, he needed them now.

"You've searched this apartment? Everywhere?"

"Yeah. Twice. I lifted rugs, I looked in the toilet, I emptied bottles. Nothing."

"Did you watch her get ready to leave the morning she disappeared?"

"Yeah. Except for when I went to get coffee. But, she didn't go anywhere while I was gone."

"How do you know?"

"I asked the doorman. He said she didn't go out at all, until she left to go to the party."

"So, she could have taken them with her then."

"Yeah. Except I watched her pack her bag. At the time, I was just curious what she was taking. I didn't even think she'd have the jewels. I saw her put everything in it. No jewels. She didn't even go near her jewelry box."

"You're an idiot. Of course she took them with her. She had to realize how much they were worth." Gustav was remembering what Sami told him on the yacht. She told him she gave them back to her boyfriend. That was a lie. Just like the lie she texted to Petrov. She didn't lose them. Unless, Petrov was lying to him and he had already sold them. Only one way to find out.

Gustav picked up his handgun and shot at Petrov's kneecap. The muffled sound of the silenced shot was nothing compared to the scream coming from Petrov.

"What the hell did you do that for? I'm bleeding to death. Help me."

"One last time. Where are they? She didn't lose them. She told me she gave them back to you."

"What? When? I don't have them. What are you talking about?" Petrov had a hard time concentrating and a harder time talking. Blood continued to run down his leg. He grimaced.

"Once more. What did you do with them?"

Petrov was writhing in pain, clutching his knee. He shook his head.

Gustav had had enough. He'd check the apartment once he finished him off. He pointed to Petrov's chest and shot. He fell back onto the sofa, blood everywhere. Calmly and thoroughly, Gustav went about searching the apartment. Bedding was ripped off, closets emptied, drawers dumped. He checked the freezer, the microwave, and the top shelves in all the closets. Her computer was easily accessed, but didn't get him information on the dia-monds. One last time through her apartment, he double-checked bookshelves and the pantry.

He found nothing. Disgusted, he kicked the unmoving Petrov on his way out of the apartment, found the thermostat, and low-ered the temperature.

"Bitch lied to me. She must have sold them. Unless, she really did have them in her purse.

"Now, I've got to figure out what to tell my buyer." His phone buzzed with an incoming message from another buyer, and he nodded as he read it. "Good. This buyer wants to meet about some of the other diamonds. That's doable. Now, to work on finding the big pieces. Maybe she really did sell them before she met me on the yacht. But, who would she know with that kind of money?"

He exited the apartment, looked up and down the hall, and locked the door behind him. "It will be awhile before anyone finds him. Good riddance."

Once back downstairs, he briefly visited with the security guard, assuring him everything was in working order.

# Thirteen

**BACK AT HIS** condo, Gustav launched into a tirade. Nothing about the visit to Sami's apartment went the way it should have. There was nothing there, and Petrov was of no help. The worst part of it all . . . he still didn't have his diamonds.

"Where the hell are they?" Furious at Petrov and at Sami, he paced the condo. "Enough, already. This isn't helping. I need a plan."

He had managed to get his hands on the guest list from the party when he was there. "Maybe someone I didn't know bought them from Petrov. But, what did he do with the money? And, why would he still be hanging around if he had that kind of money?

"Okay. I should at least take a look at this list."

He started by crossing off names of those he knew wouldn't be buyers, and making a list of those who might have been potential buyers for something high end like the ring, bracelets, and earrings. Even if they didn't pay top dollar, the buyer would still need to have available cash. And, lots of it. Nothing stood out. No one fit the bill. He was no closer than when he started. "Damn." Wadding up the list, he threw it across the room.

"There is absolutely no way she could have sold them. She didn't have time. Furthermore, who would a lowly model know with that much cash? Even if she did come across a buyer, where's

38

the money? It wasn't in her bank account." He'd already hacked into Sami's bank account using the information he took from her apartment and her computer. She hadn't made any deposits, and she wasn't wealthy. "My gut tells me Petrov was the one who sold them. But, when and where? And, where is the cash? Why wouldn't he admit it?"

Deep in thought with more questions than answers, he worked over the puzzle in his mind, coming to no solutions. When his phone buzzed with a text from his buyer from China, Mr. Kim, sweat started to form on his brow. In the whole world, he was the one guy Gustav didn't want to mess with. He sent a quick, short text back, telling him he had come down with a terrible flu and would have to postpone their meeting. He said he had just come from the hospital and would have to get back to him in a few days.

Then he sent a text to the other buyer, the one who had contacted him for some of the other pieces. He set up a meeting in a restaurant where he was confident it would be safe.

"Something has to go right."

# $\mathcal{F}$ourteen

IN THE PACIFIC Heights area, another conversation concerning diamonds was taking place.

Clark and Marta discussed more about the undercover job she was going to help Clark with. "Ian has reliable intel from one informant and more from another source, and is positive this thief is Gustav Janssen, who has had ties to every type of underworld scum they know about. He's bad news all the way around. Not many people know his name. They only know him by Gus or Mr. J. He might have a couple more aliases, too.

"He often makes multiple deals, and kills those he doesn't like. In fact, Interpol is trying to pin several murders on him. They've been close a couple of times, but he manages to slip away. It's like no one remembers what he looks like.

"Bottom line. He's a professional thief. And, a killer. Ian really wants this guy.

"I'm serious." Clark took Marta's hand and looked at her. "This is not a mandatory role for you. If you are at all concerned, you need to let me know. I already told Ian I don't like having you involved. Understand?"

Marta nodded as she processed everything Clark had told her.

Clark watched her face and continued. "Apparently, Ian's informant has been close enough to him to give a reasonable description. He's tall, at least six-three, and he's about 50, but often disguises his age. In fact, he loves disguises. The informant has bought stolen jewels from him and has had some other dealings. But, that's all we know for now."

His phone buzzed with a text. "It's Ian. He set up the meeting with Gustav, or who we're hoping is Gustav. I'm the buyer, and you're my girlfriend. We need to meet the rest of the team downtown in an hour to plan our stories, get our backgrounds in place, and go over everything. Now's the time to back out if you want to. You are not required to do this."

"No. I'm good. I'll be with you, and you look like you need a high-maintenance girlfriend anyway." Marta smiled and kissed Clark.

Clark chuckled. "Then, let's get ready to go."

# Fifteen

IN ANOTHER PART of San Francisco, Detective Karla O'Rourke was getting ready to head to the same task force meeting as Clark and Marta when her doorbell rang. Looking out, she noticed her regular mailman standing there. Opening her door, the mailman greeted her and handed her a large envelope. "Hate to bother you, Miss O'Rourke, but I got an envelope with postage due on it. Thought I'd bring it up to you instead of making you go downtown. Plus, it's kind of beat up, and I wanted to make sure everything was okay with it."

"Thanks." She took the envelope, noticed it was from her sister, and wondered why she'd send her an envelope. "I'll open it now if you want me to. That way you'll know if something is broken. It is funny she didn't just bring it to me, though."

She took the package to the kitchen counter, grabbed a scissors, and carefully cut the end off while the mailman waited by the front door. Tissue paper, a piece of paper with some scribbles on it, and something heavy wrapped in a scarf slid out onto the counter. Unfolding the scarf, she gasped and slid the contents out of sight.

"Is there any way you can tell me when and where this was mailed?" She brought the empty envelope to him.

"Just a minute. Let me pull up the tracking number." He took his small reader-like device out of his pocket and scanned the bar code on the envelope. "Looks like it was mailed two days ago at the post office in Sausalito. It could have been the day before, and they didn't actually put it into the system before then. That happens if it gets placed in the box right after they've emptied it. Anything broken?"

"No. No, everything is good. Thanks." She paid him the postage due amount and took the envelope back as he started to walk away.

"Okay. I'll just note it was delivered. Have a good day." He waved as he walked down the hall toward the elevator.

Quickly she shut the door and went back to the counter to read the scribbles on the note. It was her sister's handwriting, but more jumbled than usual. *Keep these safe. Going for a ride. I think he stole these. I'll tell you about the ring. It's a wow, but I got it so it's safe. Later. S*

"What the hell did you get into, Sami?" She picked up the earrings, noticing how the light danced off the round cut diamonds. Then, she picked up one of the bracelets. "Whoa, this is no lightweight trinket." The other bracelet was smaller, with square cut diamonds and emeralds. Their brilliance seemed to light up her entire condo. "These have got to be real, the way they look. Who the hell would give this kind of jewelry to Sami? And, why and who did she think stole them? What ring? I wonder. Could these be related in any way to the task force Interpol just set up? Those pieces were stolen in Paris, according to Ian. But, he thinks they're here now. And, these certainly fit the bill as spectacular items.

"But, how did Sami wind up with them? Where is she? And, why send them to me?" She looked in the envelope again, re-read the note, and smoothed out the scarf. "There's no ring here. The envelope was sealed, so it couldn't have fallen out. She does say she's got it. Knowing her, she's got it on her. She always likes to keep things close."

Deciding she needed to show these to the task force and to Ian, Karla wrapped everything back into the envelope, stuck it in her oversized purse, strapped on her weapon, and headed out the door.

# $\mathcal{S}$ixteen

**ALONG THE PACIFIC** Ocean, at the northwest corner of San Francisco, is the Golden Gate National Recreation Area. Within it lies the Land's End Trail which offers hikers, casual walkers, and photographers stunning views of the iconic Golden Gate Bridge and the wind-swept Cyprus trees, as well as access to the ruins of the Sutro Baths.

Where the spectacular, pounding waves meet the rocky shoreline, the resulting vistas are worth the effort to get there. That's why two hikers, Tom and Marc, decided this was the perfect day to make the trek. Tom had a new camera and Marc was along for the exercise. It was going to be a wonderful outing.

But, it turned out quite differently.

They had walked all 112 steps down the Coastal Trail to the Mile Rock Beach Lookout and Tom was setting up his tripod and camera equipment at a favorite spot when Marc spotted a towel floating among the rocks just below them. It seemed to be stuck on something. "That looks like a towel someone must have left. I'll go get it."

Slowly, he made his way over the wet rocks, being careful not to get swept away by the incoming waves. Not only did the towel create an unwanted backdrop, but neither of them liked to see garbage of any kind along the beach and rocks.

He grabbed it, but it didn't budge. Squatting down, he stepped closer and pulled harder, freeing the towel from the rocks. "Oh. My. God." For a few seconds, he was paralyzed with shock. Then, as soon as he could breathe, he dropped the towel and turned to Tom. "Call 911. I'm going to throw up."

About an hour later, fire and rescue teams and police had brought the body up to a waiting medical examiner's van in the parking lot and taped off the area. Several officers were sifting through the rocks below, looking for clues as to why the body was there. Tom and Marc had been questioned and were being attended to for shock. As the ambulance and van pulled out of the lot, Marc looked at the officer still with them.

"What's going to happen? I mean, do we need to do anything? God, I can't get that image out of my mind. That poor girl. I mean, it was a girl, right? She had on a dress and had long hair. But, she looked so . . ." His voice trailed off as the image was still fresh in his mind. He was still pale, but shaking less than he had for the past hour. Tom kept rubbing his shoulders and shaking his head.

The sympathetic officer nodded. He knew all too well what these two were going through. Their brains hadn't even begun to process it all, and it would take time for them to get the grisly image out of their minds. "We'll do an investigation, look at missing person reports, and try to identify the body. The two of you don't need to do anything more. I can take you to be checked out further by a physician, if you want. If not, you have my card and can call me anytime. This isn't easy for you, I know. Please don't hesitate to talk to one of us or some professional about the events. Okay?"

The officer in charge had taken their statements and collected their information. An EMT had checked over both hikers.

They looked at each other, nodded, and assured the officer they would be okay, once everything sunk in.

Evidence was still being collected from the trail and the rocks as they packed up their equipment and left.

# Seventeen

**DOWNTOWN, EVERYONE HAD** assembled for the task force meeting, and Ian had been conferenced in via Skype. Introductions were made, as Marta and two other people were new. Marta was the only non-law enforcement person present, but Ian explained why she was there. If Clark deemed some part of this as too risky, Marta would no longer be involved. She and Detective Karla O'Rourke smiled at each other.

Karla mentioned to Ian she had something she wanted him to see. He asked her to wait a few minutes, as he wanted to bring everyone up to speed about the theft of the jewelry.

He had additional information from Paris, including a time of death for Matilda and for the nephew, which he relayed to the group. "This confirms the fact that the nephew was killed prior to Matilda. These are the facts as we know them. The nephew was shot and his body dumped along a remote stretch of the river. Matilda died from blunt force trauma, most likely from a statue bust which the police found at her mansion. No prints on it at all.

"The only other prints found at the mansion were those of the nephew, Matilda, and the housekeeper, who just came in once a week. These were in places you would expect they would have touched. All alarms inside the mansion had been disabled. From the front door security camera, it was noticed that a workman from the alarm company had been there three days prior to Matilda's death. He didn't look at the camera, but his van was seen driving away by a neighbor. At the time, the neighbor didn't think anything of it. But, when the police questioned him this past week, he mentioned it. When police visited the alarm company, they had no record of being at that address in the past several months. To further the puzzle, one of their vans had been reported stolen three days prior to that.

"We asked the alarm company to check the alarms from their end, and they found they were not working. Upon further investigation, they discovered how they had been disabled. Apparently, someone knew what they were doing." Ian paused and then continued with more information.

"This is what we have learned about the diamonds and jewelry. We're sure it all would have weighed around 30 or 40 pounds, according to records we obtained from their foundation. The thief or thieves could have easily removed all of it in a couple of bags or boxes. We are assuming each piece was either in a jeweler's wrap or its own box as those were not left behind. Still, it wouldn't have been difficult to take it all.

"Among all the spectacular pieces were two special bracelets, which had been in her family for over 150 years. The diamonds were close to flawless, according to the insurance company. One bracelet had matching earrings and one had some emeralds in with the diamonds. Each bracelet had enough diamonds to create quite the buzz. Their value comes from the quality of the diamonds, plus their history. Part of that history is a little fuzzy and possibly not all true, but Matilda's attorney filled us in as best he could.

"The larger bracelet, the one with the most diamonds, is reported to have been acquired as payment from a gambling debt. This was most likely over a hundred years ago. Her great-grandfather was quite the gambler. The family story says he and another man were at odds over some trade deal, and they made a bet. They played one hand of cards. Winner take all. He won, and the other man needed to pay him a huge amount to settle the debt. That man, the one who lost, tossed the bracelet to her great-grandfather, and then wanted to do a double-or-nothing bet. Matilda's great-grandfather wanted no part of that and took the bracelet as payment. This infuriated the other man, who vowed to get it back, regardless of what it took. Then, in a strange twist, the legend says the loser of the bracelet killed himself that day, rather than be disgraced in his family by losing it. Kind of a weird tale, if you ask me.

"The attorney doesn't even know if the story is true or if it's just a legend. Apparently, Matilda told him her great-grandfather was good at making up stories, especially when it came to publicity. And, none of the diamonds or other jewelry has ever been stolen. In fact, there's never been an attempt in all these years. So, it could be just that. A story." Ian took a breath, then continued.

"The other amazing piece was a 15 carat, nearly flawless, round, brilliant-cut diamond ring. It's valued at well over forty million dollars due to its cut and age. There are more rings and other pieces, of course, but these are the most notable." Ian paused. "One reason we're positive at least some of these jewels are there in San Francisco, is some footage SFPD obtained from a security guard at a party last weekend. The short version is that the guard, who is actually an SFPD detective, recognized a known jewel thief at the party. His date was wearing what we have identified as one of the stolen bracelets. The thief stole another bracelet while the guard was watching, but he and his date left before we could nab them. We've positively ID'd the thief as Petrov Smit. Photos of both him and his date are in the files in front of you. Take a look and let me know if you recognize either of them."

Karla glanced at the photos in the folder and closed her eyes. "Damn." Everyone turned to look at her.

"Karla, earlier you said you had something. Is it related?"

She sighed. "Ian, I do have something, and I know the woman with the thief." She reached for her bag as her phone buzzed. "This morning an envelope was delivered to me." She paused as she pulled out the envelope. Laying it on the table so Ian could see it, she opened it. "This is what was in it."

Gasps could be heard around the room as the sensational bracelets and earrings took center stage. No one spoke for a few seconds. Ian was first. "Whoa. Clark, take a close look at those, and tell me if they're what I think they are. Detective, who touched the envelope besides you?"

"It was delivered by my regular mailman, so probably a whole bunch of people touched it. He brought it to me personally because there was postage due, and he'd seen that the envelope was a little beat up and wanted to make sure everything was okay inside."

"Did he see what was in it?"

"No. I opened it out of his sight and then told him it was all okay before he left."

"Do you think he had any idea?"

"No, I really don't."

Clark had been looking at the jewelry. "What about this note, Karla? Do you know what it means? Do you know who it's from?"

"Yeah. It's from my sister. She's the woman in the photo. The thief's date."

# Eighteen

"OKAY, I THINK you'd better start at the beginning and tell us about your sister."

"Sure thing." Just as she started to tell the group about Sami, one of the other SFPD detective's phone rang. He looked at the number and excused himself. Karla had just mentioned Sami was her younger sister who had been modeling since she was a teenager. Their parents were killed several years ago, and Karla had been both mother and big sister to Sami. The detective walked back into the room.

"Sorry to interrupt, but there's an issue. Karla, we need you to come with us."

"What? Why? Can't another detective fill in until I'm finished with this?"

"I'm sorry to tell you like this, Karla, but a body was found this morning. One of the EMTs recognized the body as a model, one his girlfriend likes. She says the model goes by the name of Sami. I think she's your sister."

Karla stood up and then sat back down. "What the hell?"

Ian spoke from the screen. "Okay, everybody, let's reconvene in three hours. Karla, please do what you need to do. And, if you want off this task force, just let me know. This is a difficult time for you, so don't hesitate to ask.

"Clark, will you take the envelope with the jewelry to our lab? We need to be sure these are the stolen items. Get back to me within the hour.

"I'll see everybody back here in three hours."

# Nineteen

**GUSTAV WAS BECOMING** more frustrated with each breath. He had nothing. Petrov was dead. Sami was dead. Where were his diamonds?

He shook his head. "I don't get it. She wore them one day, put them in her jewelry box at night, and came onto the boat the next day. What the hell did she do with them?" He stood up and paced. "Or, did she really give them back to Petrov, and he lied to me? Wouldn't be the first time. But, if she gave them back to him, what the hell did he do with them? If he had sold them, he wouldn't have been hanging around her apartment waiting for her to return. He's not that nice.

"I think she stashed them somewhere when he wasn't looking, and was going to get them after our little boat ride. But, where? She didn't seem like the brilliant type. And, they weren't in her apartment. I'm positive about that. So, did she pack them up and take them with her? I know they weren't in her purse and she wasn't wearing them. She must have stopped somewhere. But, where?

"Damn. I'm getting nowhere."

After a couple more hours of looking online for black market sites that had diamonds for sale, he was still no closer to finding out what had happened to the two bracelets, earrings, and ring. Then, he spent the next hour removing more of the diamonds, emeralds, and rubies from their settings. He knew he could sell the platinum and gold for top dollar separately. He left the rings alone. All eight of them, minus the one he really wanted.

"That ring. It is my nest egg. I have to have it."

Locking everything up, he decided to turn on the news while he had a glass of wine and thought about what he was going to tell his Chinese buyer. Mr. Kim did not accept changes in agreements. There were too many stories of people who had crossed him and ended up in pieces, or just never to be heard from again. This was not going to happen to him. "Finding that bracelet is the only way I can deal with him."

He paced while the news reporter stood in front of The Golden Gate Bridge, talking about somebody drowning. He didn't pay much attention.

# $\mathcal{T}$wenty

KARLA AND HER partner, Detective Scotty Smith, made their way to the morgue. "Are you ready for this? I mean, this could be your sister. Are you okay?"

Karla nodded and took a deep breath. "Yeah. Let's do this and get it over with." She took another breath, letting it out slowly, as the elevator stopped at the basement level. She looked at Scotty. "Now I know what other families feel like when I bring them here." They made their way down the hall and through the outer room to the double set of doors, just outside the morgue. From inside, the medical examiner unlocked them, and they silently opened.

Entering the cold, sterile room with the nose-tingling, antiseptic smells, and ugly tile floor weren't the only things that gave Karla the shivers. Immediately, her gaze went to the draped body lying on the stainless steel table in the center of the room. The medical examiner, who she knew so well, came forward and gave her a hug. "I'm so sorry."

She smiled as he stepped back. "I'm ready."

Slowly, he lifted the sheet from the body's face. Tears crept down Karla's face as she took in the familiar red hair, now in a matted disarray, and the perfect, flawless complexion, now marred by water, rocks, and death. "She wouldn't want anybody to see her like this. Her hair's a mess. She has no make-up on. Yet, to me, she's still beautiful."

She took a huge breath and looked at the M.E. "Yeah. It's her. Positive. No need for DNA."

The medical examiner re-covered her face with the sheet. "Since the two of you look so much alike, I was afraid this was your sister."

"How did she die? Or, do you know yet?"

"As you know, this has not been confirmed, and I wouldn't tell anyone but you this early. Preliminary cause of death was a stab wound to the throat. It appears she may have bled out before she ended up in the ocean. We'll know more after I finish the autopsy and get tissue samples to the lab. I'll keep you informed."

Karla nodded. "Do you know when?"

"Not yet. I can put a TOD after the autopsy and after the lab gets back to me. With the body in the cold Pacific water, it's harder to give an exact time."

"Can you guess?"

The M.E. smiled at her. "I know you want all the details. I would too, if I were you. I'd venture to guess, and it's only a guess, that she died possibly two to four days ago. But, don't take that as positive. Let me get some more results. Okay?"

"Sure. Thanks, Doc. This might help. She was supposed to meet me for lunch two days ago and never showed up. That's the last I heard from her. Also, two days ago, or possibly three, she mailed an envelope to me. The mailman wasn't exactly sure on the date."

"Good to know. That might narrow things down a bit for us."

# Twenty-One

**KARLA COMPOSED HERSELF** after they left the morgue. Turning to Scotty she said, "That was the hardest, scariest thing I've ever had to do. Now, I'm mad, and I want answers. She was my only family, and she didn't deserve to end up this way. Let's get back to the task force and see what Clark found out about the jewelry she sent to me."

"You don't have to do this, you know. You can take some time to organize your thoughts and see what you want to do."

"I know. But, obviously Sami was mixed up in this jewelry mess somehow. I can't quit. And, I can't give up on her."

"Yeah, I figured. Let's go."

"After the meeting I need to get to her apartment and see what I find. Will you come with me?"

"Of course. But, you know you can't be in on the investigation?"

Everyone had reassembled and told Karla how sorry they were. Ian reiterated the fact she didn't have to do this, but wasn't surprised when she told him she was determined to find out all she could about the jewelry, Sami's death, and how they fit together. "Because I know they fit. Sami didn't have that kind of jewelry, she didn't run around with thieves, and she had straightened out her life in the past few years. There was a reason she had those jewels, and there was a reason she sent them to me. Let's find out."

"Was she always a model?"

"For many years, Marta. Starting in her early teens, she modeled for teen magazines, then graduated to fashion magazines and different designers. Unfortunately, she got mixed up in some porn-type publications for about a year when she was just starting out. Once she realized what they wanted her do, she came to me, and we got her out of that. Fast."

"Do you think she still had contacts in that world? I mean, could someone from her past life have given her the jewelry and wanted her to do something which wasn't exactly above board? We've looked at her note. She mentions someone stole them. What does your gut tell you? How do you think she knew they were stolen? She also says she's going for a ride. Any idea where or with whom? Was it along the coast, do you think? And, what about a ring? She said she has it. What does that mean to you?"

"All the same questions I have, Ian. I've been thinking back over our last conversation. We were supposed to meet for lunch. That's when I met Marta and Clark, at the Cliff House Restaurant. She stood me up and didn't let me know why. Now I wonder if this was why. At the time, she hadn't mentioned anything about jewelry or going for a ride, so I just don't know.

"I don't really know all of her friends, either. I've met some of the other models, but I don't think she had a big group of friends. She was always hanging out with me. I seriously doubt she had gotten back into the porn world. It really left a mark on her. In fact, she had just started talking about helping young, teen-age models learn about porn and what it does to you and your career.

"After we're done here, Detective Smith and I are going to Sami's apartment. Maybe we'll find something there."

"Karla, you can't be on that investigation. Let our detectives do it. I'll have them meet you there so you can do a quick walk-through. But, then you have to leave. Okay? You know that." George, Karla's boss, put his hand on her arm.

"Yeah, boss, I know. I just want to see her apartment. I know where she keeps her jewelry and thought there might be more there."

"Wait. Got it? Okay?"

Karla nodded as Ian addressed the group. "The rest of us need to concentrate on the jewelry first. SFPD will bring us up to speed on her death."

# Twenty-Two

**GUSTAV WAS STILL** frantically working on figuring out where his jewelry was. His efforts yielded no results. He was frustrated and mad. And, scared. Mr. Kim's most recent text was hanging over his head, creating a major distraction.

At this point, he had to assume Petrov lied to him. "He probably hid them right after Sami left. I shouldn't have killed him and maybe he would have told me where they were. It's a good thing I have the rest of the diamonds to sell to other clients. There's no way I want to call to Mr. Kim and let him know anything, but at this point I don't know what else to do. I could offer a deal on some of the other diamonds. Maybe that would appease him.

"Then, I'll have to disappear before he can find me. I have no intention of being one of his casualties."

He thought about those diamonds sitting in his safe. "At least I'm meeting with another buyer. I'll just jack up those prices and make my money there. Then, if I don't find the others, I'll leave town. Fast."

He started working out the details of that meeting. Because he had already checked out the credentials of his buyer, he knew he was meeting with someone who bought questionable diamonds on the international black market, and who had had some trouble with the law in the past year. What he didn't know, was that these credentials were totally fabricated. Clark was the buyer, posing as a Mr. Marsh. His new identity was well documented and created no red flags for Gustav.

The meeting place was determined by Gustav. This time, he picked a busy, family restaurant in the Little Italy neighborhood of San Francisco. He would be wearing one of his disguises. When Mr. Marsh, the buyer, showed him the down payment, he would show only a small portion of the diamonds. Once Marsh wired the rest of the money to Gustav's account, he would notify him where he could pick up the jewels. Marsh wouldn't see him again. This is the way he worked.

Satisfied everything was how he wanted it, he sent a text to Mr. Marsh with explicit instructions. He was to come alone at the appointed time and ask for Mr. Johanssen, a name he only used occasionally. Once the transaction took place, Marsh would then leave the restaurant ahead of Gustav. No diamonds would be released until full payment was received in his account. These were the terms if the buyer wanted a deal.

He also had a Plan B, in case he needed it. He often did.

He knew he would be at the restaurant a full hour ahead of time to watch for anyone suspicious. He didn't want any body-guards or trigger-happy thugs associated with Mr. Marsh to plant themselves there. He had a routine, and it had worked for more than a decade. Different city; same plan.

"As soon as I get these sold, I'm heading out. Time to move on and sell the rest later. Mr. Kim can go to hell, for all I care."

# Twenty-Three

IAN GAVE ASSIGNMENTS to the task force. He was going on the assumption the seller was Gustav, as intel had recently reported Mr. J, Mr. Johanssen, and Gustav were all the same person. Reports from his informants confirmed Gustav had diamonds for sale, but they couldn't confirm if they were the rest of the ones stolen in Paris. He was hoping Clark would come away with some of them, and then they would know what they were dealing with.

"Okay, people. Lots of assumptions here. Based on previous dealings, we know he's a master of disguises, which puts us all at a disadvantage. We have no idea what he will look like on that day. If he is the one in our security camera footage from the mansion, he's a big guy. That might work to a disadvantage for him. Otherwise, his age is around 50. And, you all know he can disguise that.

"The restaurant he's chosen is a busy place, probably by his design. He thinks no one will remember him if there are a lot of people around and a lot of things happening. We also have to assume he's been here before and knows the layout.

"We also assume he's going to watch everyone in the place carefully. He's not stupid. In fact, he's quite brilliant and can probably spot one of us a mile away. So, we need to be extra careful and we need to blend. What we don't know is when he will get there. If he's there for a while, you are going to have to adjust to that.

I know I don't need to tell you, but there can be no red flags. Don't overstay your visit.

"This guy could be from the Paris heist. He says he's selling diamonds, but who knows where he got them, if they're actually the ones from Paris, or if he was the thief. This could be a totally different group of diamonds, and we could walk away with nothing from the Paris heist.

"Like I said, lots of assumptions.

"Clark, you're Mr. Marsh, and you and Marta are going to be a couple. He's probably already checked you out and knows you are a ruthless buyer who's had some legal issues. Your credentials are all in place. Marta, so far he knows nothing about you. Your credentials say your name is Marie. If he checks after the fact, he'll find out you're a socialite with an appetite for jewelry. Take the packets home and study them. He specifically said you are to come alone, Clark, so you're going to have to make him believe Marta goes where you go.

"George, you're one of the sommeliers. You look Italian and you know wine. The owner has been contacted and thinks you are prepping for a show which will be filmed later in the month at their restaurant. He thinks you're important, and he knows he has to keep this a secret or the film company won't pick them. He has read your bio. Have fun."

"Thanks, Ian. Certainly better than being homeless, like my last assignment. Not every day the chief will let me drink on the job."

"Right. Karla and Scotty, you're tourists. You need to dress as such and act like this is your first time in San Francisco. Have a hard time making up your minds about food and wine. Drag it out as long as you can without causing any issues. You can read your bios and particulars in your folders.

"Roger and I discussed timing issues. This will depend on how long Gustav has been there. We don't want anything to give him cause for alarm or have him abandon this meeting. Roger is going to get there fairly early. He's a businessman waiting for his client. Roger, you can fill them in after I'm finished.

"Stu and Angie, you're professionals stopping in for a glass of wine and catching up. Talk, laugh, and show photos, etc.

"Charles, I need you at the bar, nursing a drink. There's a nice mirror, so you should be able to see what's going on.

"Douglas, you get to be a waiter. You've been cleared and ready to start. You'll be following another real waiter around as part of your training."

"Hey, I get to be a waiter, and Charles gets to drink. What's up with that?" Everyone chuckled.

"Well, I have your file in front of me, and it says you waited tables in college." Douglas nodded.

"Yeah, and I drank in college." Charles held up his water bottle as a salute. More laughter.

"Okay. Everybody has their folders. The meet is tomorrow. We'll have one last meeting here before then. Any questions? Karla, remember only to take a brief look at your sister's apartment. And, if you want off at any time, just let me know. Okay?"

"Sure thing. Scotty and I are going there next."

"Wait for SFPD. Got it?" George echoed what Ian had told her.

"Yeah, boss. I got it. I just want to see her place one last time."

# Twenty-Four

**KARLA AND SCOTTY** pulled up to the apartment
building where Sami lived. "Wow. Nice place. Do you have a key?"

"Yeah, I do. And, Ivan, the doorman knows me. I wouldn't
come here often, though, as she usually came to my place. Recently
rent has gone so sky high, she was thinking of moving out of here
and to a smaller community. She was getting more and more work
that wasn't local, so it was beginning to make less sense to spend
the kind of money she did on rent here." Karla sighed as they
walked up to the doorman.

"Hey, Karla, we need to wait for the rest of the guys from
SFPD. Remember?"

"They'll be here. Let's talk to Ivan while we wait."

Ivan hugged Karla and they chatted for a while before he told
Karla he hadn't seen Sami in a few days. Karla looked at Scotty.

"Ivan, we have some bad news. This is my partner, Detective
Scotty Smith. We've just come from the morgue where I had to
identify Sami's body."

Ivan paled, took off his hat, and shook his head. "I don't
understand. She was fine when she left here a few days ago."

"I'm sorry to have to tell you, but she drowned. Some hikers
found her body by Land's End."

"What was she doing there? You know she doesn't swim. And, she's too pretty to be out there. I don't get it."

"I know. We don't have all the details yet. Some people from SFPD are coming, and Detective Smith and I are going to look in her apartment. I'll have to come back later to clean it out, and I'll notify the landlord."

"What about her friend? I don't like to call him her boyfriend. He wasn't in her class. He was just using her. I know it."

"What friend? Do you know his name?" Karla had her pad and pen out and was taking notes.

"I think she introduced him to me as Peter something. He had shifty eyes and wouldn't look at me. I tell ya, he was just using her. Probably up to no good."

"Okay. Do you know the last time you saw him? Did they leave together lately? What can you tell me about him and about them together?" Karla was in her full investigative, detective mode.

Detective Smith put his hand on Karla's arm. "Wait. They need to do this, not you."

Karla nodded as Ivan put his hand on his forehead.

"Well, let me think. It was at least two or three days ago when Miss Sami left. By herself. She was all dressed up and excited. Told me she was going to a party on some guy's yacht. She looked so pretty." Ivan paused, as if remembering her that day. "She asked me if I liked her new shoes. They were ones with those skinny heels. Don't know how she could walk on land, let alone on a boat."

Karla smiled and nodded as she wrote. "Did she say where or what she was going to do?"

"No. Just a party. I didn't ask questions. She was so bubbly. I should have asked where she was going. I'm sorry." Ivan looked like he had the weight of the world on his shoulders.

Karla patted his arm. "Ivan, don't worry. You couldn't have stopped her anyway. When she wanted to party, she partied. Now, when did she come home?"

"That's just it. I don't remember seeing her come home. At all." He shook his head. "No. I haven't seen her since."

"Okay. What about her friend? Peter, is it?"

"Yeah, him I've seen. But, come to think of it, not lately. Maybe he's looking for her. Or, he cleaned out her stuff and sold it and moved on. Maybe Sami chased him to Land's End, and he killed her."

"Whoa. Let's not jump to conclusions, Ivan. When did you last see him?" Detective Smith had also been taking notes as Ivan was talking.

"Well. He went out for coffee the morning Sami left. Then, later that morning he came down and asked me if Sami had gone out while he was getting coffee. That was weird. He wasn't gone that long. The next day I think I saw him come in the building, but I was on the phone with a fire inspector. That's the last I remember. But, you know I'm only here until 7 o'clock. He could have left at night and be long gone by now."

Two police cruisers pulled up and officers got out. They joined Karla and Scotty.

"Thanks, Ivan. We're going to look through her apartment now. We'll let you know if we need anything. Thanks for all of your help."

Ivan nodded as they went toward the two elevators. He rubbed at tears slowly running down his face.

# Twenty-Five

**"I THINK IT** really hit him hard. Poor guy."

"Yeah. He's been here for years, and I think he really connects with the people in the building. They're more than just tenants to him. They're his friends. I hated to tell him she was dead, but on the other hand, I didn't want him to see it on the news. Did you catch that he said she was going to a party on a yacht? I wonder if that's what she meant when she said she was going for a ride."

They stopped at the door to Sami's apartment, Karla used her key to open the door, and stepped back to let the others in. Immediately, they were hit with a sickening smell and cold air. All four immediately pulled their weapons and went in, sweeping the area, to the left and to the right. Noticing the body on the sofa, the drying blood, and the smell, they knew they didn't have to get an ambulance here quickly.

"Clear." All four echoed the signal.

Putting their weapons away, Karla first touched the neck of the body. "No pulse. What do ya bet it's her friend, Peter?"

"Yeah. Good bet. Damn, it's cold in here. Wonder if that was by design so no one would smell the body?"

"Probably. And, if so, then we're dealing with a professional. I was thinking we could hang meat in here as cold as it is. You call it in. I'm going to look around."

Scotty called the medical examiner and George, Karla's and his boss, to let him know what they found. George reminded him to get Karla out of there. He couldn't have her on the case of her sister and mess up something, especially with a dead body in her apartment. Scotty assured him he would do that.

One of the officers motioned to Karla. "Detective, don't touch anything. I think you need to leave. Okay? I know I don't need to tell you, but be careful. You don't want Sami to be a suspect here."

"One minute. I just want to see if things look like Sami would have left them." Karla started toward her bedroom, an officer following. "Detective. Let's go."

Karla gasped when she saw the trashed bedroom, but turned around and went back downstairs to talk to Ivan to let him know what was happening. Clearly, he was still distraught. They talked for over an hour about Sami, but Karla was careful to just listen as he told her stories about her sister. "She was such a good person."

As the gurney came out of the elevator, Ivan got all teary-eyed again. "I didn't even like him. But, who would kill him? It's not like he was a bad guy or anything. Just a leech on Sami." He started to cry again.

"Ivan, can you call your boss? He needs to know what's going on, and I think you should talk to one of our physicians. Can you do that?"

Ivan nodded and made a phone call. "He says he's coming here and that I can go home after he gets here."

Scotty and Karla left Ivan with one of the EMTs who had pulled up with the Medical Examiner's van. Scotty turned to Karla. "Find anything?"

"I just took a quick look. Certainly looks like the apartment was trashed, like somebody was looking for something. Shampoo and perfume bottles are emptied in the sink and thrown on the floor, toilet lid is off, closet has been emptied onto the floor, shoes everywhere. It's a disaster."

"Was Sami neat or was she messy?"

"Totally a neat freak."

"You didn't move anything, did you?"

"Nope. I was good. Just looked and didn't move a thing."

"Okay. Let's head downtown."

# Twenty-Six

**SEVERAL HOURS LATER** Sami's apartment had
been processed and the other detectives were meeting with Scotty
and Karla. "We have all the photos we need, Karla. Everything has
been dusted for prints, and the apartment checked over. Chief said
you can now go back in and look at her things. Don't take anything
yet, but you can move stuff. We've been over that apartment with
a fine tooth comb looking for jewelry per Chief's request. Found
nothing special. Just some things in her jewelry box that look like
normal stuff. Let us know if you have any questions."

"Okay. Thanks, guys. I think I'll stop there on my way home. I
have a big day tomorrow."

Karla headed to Sami's apartment, let herself in, and just
stood in the middle of the chaos. "Sami would be so upset at this
mess." A small sob escaped and she covered her mouth. Tears
silently fell on her cheeks. "Oh, dear Sami. What did you get into?
Was the jewelry part of it? What happened?" Slowly, she made her
way through the apartment, making a list of things she wanted.
She'd give this list to the chief, then she would come and box up
those things to take home.

The clothes and shoes could be donated, the furniture taken
to a shelter, and most everything else taken somewhere where
it could be used. Sami didn't have anything valuable, except for

her portfolio of modeling photographs, her laptop computer, and her purses. She loved expensive purses, and Karla found nine of them in her closet and strewn throughout her bedroom, including the one Karla had just given her for her birthday. Karla would take those and see which ones she wanted to keep, along with the portfolio. Everything else could go. She didn't even find her phone. "Guess she had that with her and it's probably at the bottom of the Pacific."

Bedding was ripped off the bed, pictures taken off the wall, and every drawer emptied out. "I noticed most of this was already done before we got here. Somebody was looking for something. Probably not the guy who was shot. So, who? And, what did he find?" She walked around as she mumbled. "Wonder what they were looking for? Probably the diamonds she sent to me. Which means whoever did this didn't know she sent them to me. What a mess."

After sorting through everything in the bedroom, and finding nothing to give her any clues, she sat down on the bed. The doorbell rang.

She drew her weapon and quietly went to the door. She could see a shadow under the door, so she moved to the side, and called out. "Who's there?"

No answer, but Karla could still see the shadow. She repeated, "Who's there?"

A tiny voice answered. "It's me. Betty. Where's Sami? Who is this?"

Karla took a chance and slowly turned the knob with her left hand, pushing it open with her foot, as she held her weapon in her right hand, out of sight. Standing in the wide hallway was a middle-aged, well dressed, short woman. Looking at Karla and trying to look into the apartment at the same time, she smiled tentatively as she asked again. "Who are you? Where's Sami? May I come in?"

Not wanting her to see the apartment, Karla stepped into the doorway, partially closing the door. She stuck her weapon in the waistband of her pants, at the small of her back. "Hi, Betty. I'm Karla, Sami's sister."

Betty was still trying to see into the apartment. "Is Sami here?"

"No. She's not. Is there somewhere we can talk?"

"What about here in her apartment? I've been over to visit her a lot." She pointed to the partially closed door.

"Where do you live, Betty?"

"Right there." Turning slightly, she pointed to another door at the end of the hallway. "Is something wrong with Sami? We haven't heard from her."

Karla sighed. "Betty, I need to talk to you. But, not here at her apartment. Can we go to yours to talk?"

Nodding, she turned toward her door.

"Let me grab my purse, and I'll be right there." Karla grabbed her purse and her list, shut and locked Sami's door, and headed to Betty's.

# Twenty-Seven

BETTY HELD HER door open for Karla. Entering a spacious, similar looking apartment, Karla immediately noticed several head shots of models she recognized hanging throughout, including one of Sami. With a puzzled look on her face, she turned to Betty. "Are you a fan of models? Do you collect photos?"

Betty smiled. "You could say that. I'm the assistant, slash gofer, slash organizer, slash Betty will do it, for a modeling agency here in San Francisco. Those lovely ladies have all worked for us. Sami is especially dear to me. She's had such a hard time. But, you already know that. I hope she's not run off with that terrible photographer. I mean, he's an okay photographer. He's just a terrible person. And, he's not good for her.

"Let me get you a drink, and you can tell me where you think she is. By the way, I feel like I already know you. She talked so much about her sister." She shook her head. "Karla. Right?"

Karla nodded. "Yes, I'm Karla. And, I know Sami spoke highly of the people she worked with. As for the drink, let's sit down first. I have some bad news. Really bad news." Karla filled Betty in on some of the details about Sami, excluding the gorier ones.

Betty kept shaking her head, tears streaming down her cheeks.

"I can't believe it. She was so sweet and so talented. Who would want to do that? Are the police looking for whoever dumped her?" She sniffed.

"Why do you think she was dumped?"

"She hated swimming. Didn't you know that? She said it made her hair a mess and turned it dull. She was proud of her thick, curly, red hair. And, I know it was natural. She told me." Looking at Karla, she smiled. "It reminds me of your hair, if yours was longer."

"Yeah. I did know that about her. Betty, I have some other news. I am Sami's sister, but I am also a SFPD detective. So, in answer to your question, the police are working on her death. Would it be okay if I called my partner to come ask you some questions about Sami? I can't get too involved since she was my sister."

"Of course, dear. In fact, I can tell you about a man who called looking for her and Peter."

"Hold that thought, Betty. I need to make a phone call and get someone here."

Karla placed a call to Scotty, telling him to bring another detective and to hurry.

# Twenty-Eight

BETTY FINISHED TELLING her story to the two detectives while Karla listened. She filled them in on how she saw the relationship between Peter and Sami dissolving, gave her opinion of Peter, and told them she didn't trust him. She then explained about receiving a call from Mr. J, who said he was trying to locate them, and she told them how rude he was. "He sounded French, but he talked so fast."

She cried when she told them she gave Sami's address to him. "I should have never done that. I knew it at the time, but I did it anyway. Sami was the sweetest person. I know she had some stuff in her past because she told me about it, but she was all professional and one of the best models we had. We could send her anywhere, and she delivered.

"Now, Peter on the other hand was good at getting her to smile. But, he wasn't reliable. Too many times he just wasn't available. Never said why. Always said he had to go to Paris. He wasn't that well known as a photographer, so I'm not sure what he was doing in Paris." Betty paused to wipe her eyes.

"Oh. I remember he told me once he was going to be rich, and then he and Sami could go wherever they wanted. I didn't pay any attention to him. He was always scheming. I still don't know what she saw in him.

"And, now she's dead. Probably because of him. I hope you find that scum and give him what he deserves."

The detectives looked at Karla, and she nodded.

"Betty. The other piece of news we have for you is about Peter. He was killed in Sami's apartment." Scotty had put his hand on her shoulder as he gave her this news.

"Good. I'm glad. Well, I'm not glad he died in Sami's apartment. But, I'm glad he's gone. Oh dear. I probably shouldn't say that, should I?" She looked at all three in the room as her eyes got bigger. "You don't think Sami did it, do you? I mean, she couldn't even hurt a bug."

"Don't worry, Betty. Sami could not have killed him. We're working on his murder. Now, we want you to be careful both here and at work. Does this Mr. J person know you live in the same building as Sami?"

"No. I don't know. I may have mentioned it. Why? Do you think he had something to do with all of this?"

"We don't know yet. Let us work on all of that. We just want you to be careful. Okay?" Scotty had sat down next to Betty on her sofa and was talking to her like he would his mother. She was nodding as she listened to him. "And, Betty, will you do a favor for me?"

Betty nodded. "Of course. Anything I can do to find out how Sami died."

"Good. Go about your normal routine and don't say anything to the other models or photographers. We're going to come to the agency tomorrow to talk to those who are there. We'll contact the rest individually. But, this is important, if you remember anything, and I mean any little detail, call me right away. Something that pops into your brain might be important. Okay?"

"Okay."

"Are you going to be okay here? Do you want to stay somewhere else for tonight?"

"I'm okay. I have a good alarm and I'll be careful. I'll rack my brain for anything I may have missed in talking with the guy who called."

Scotty, Karla, and the detectives left once they heard Betty set her alarm and lock her doors.

# Twenty-Nine

**"THAT WAS TOUGH** for her. Poor lady." Scotty and Karla were at their respective cars.

"Yeah. I think I'll call her in a couple of days to see how she's doing."

"Be careful. You know Chief doesn't want you involved in this. Why don't I call her instead?"

"Thanks, Scotty. Let's do it together. I think she really liked Sami. But, then who wouldn't?"

"I just wish I knew what she was up to and where she got the jewelry. Do you really think this Peter guy gave it to her? I mean, why? Was he the one she mentioned in her note to me, the one she thought stole it? I have so many questions."

"Then, there's the caller, Mr. J. Could the mysterious Mr. J be the one Ian mentioned? That would fit, especially if we're talking about the Paris diamonds. Right?" She looked at Scotty.

"I have no idea on any of it right now. Let's tell Ian about Mr. J, and let the detectives on the case figure out what Betty knows that might help us. We need to concentrate on the jewelry and the thief. See you in the morning for the last briefing. Okay?"

"Yeah. Night."

So many thoughts and questions kept crowding into her mind as she drove home. *Where did you get the jewelry and why did you*

76

*send it to me? Is or was Peter involved? He had to be. Right? Who killed you and why? Did you really go for a ride with someone you didn't know? Who? Is that the person who killed you? You mentioned a ring. Did you have that, too? Where is it? You said it was safe. But, where? What the hell were you involved in, Sami?*

"Damn." No answers came to her.

# Thirty

**EVERYONE HAD GATHERED** for the last briefing before Clark and Marta were to meet with Mr. Johanssen.

"First, I need to fill you in on the man killed in Sami's apartment. His name was Petrov Smit and he was a small time thief, mostly jewelry. He's been on SFPD's radar off and on for about three years. They didn't have much to do with him the past few months, however, until he showed up at that party with Sami. Now, it seems like he's caught up in something that got him killed.

"SFPD is working that case, for now. They have interviewed Betty, the models, and the photographers, and are still piecing his life together. No one at the agency knew much about him, and no one knew him as Petrov Smit, either. One model mentioned he was a loner and not the best photographer she had ever worked with. I'll pass along more information when I get it."

He then finished the briefing.

"Does anyone have any questions, or is anyone uncomfortable in how this will go down?"

Roger spoke up. "Ian, I think we've all got it. Everybody will be in their places at the appointed times. One question, though. Does anybody know how long he'll be there after Clark and Marta leave the restaurant?"

"Good question. The timing all depends on how long he has been there. George and Doug, you'll be the only two who can be there early and hang around. One of you will have to notify the rest who this guy is and when he gets there. If it's early, I don't want everyone coming in at the same time. There would be no reason to hang around. We're playing things a little close for comfort, but it can't be helped this time.

"As for him leaving, again, we'll play it by ear. George and Doug, you're there for the duration, unless something funny happens. Sorry, guys.

"We're going to have to hope there's another meeting. I can't see him just handing over the diamonds to you, Clark, no matter how much money you tell him you have. I think he wants to get a feel for you and the money. We can always hope he's greedy and wants to unload them quickly.

"Okay. Good luck, everyone. We'll meet after the meeting. Stay safe."

# Thirty-One

GUSTAV ENTERED ONE of the condo's bedrooms, which he had turned into a studio for his complete set of disguises. Everything was organized. Clothing, wigs, make-up, padding, and shoes filled his specially-designed containers. Along one entire wall; mirrors. Here, he painstakingly worked on his disguise for that evening.

Since he was tall, and he didn't want anyone to realize that, he'd have to remain sitting during his exchange with Mr. Marsh. He wouldn't get up when Marsh arrived at his table and he would hunch his shoulders, making him appear older and smaller. Since he had rather large hands, he'd have to downplay those as much as possible. No placing them both on the table at the same time, and he'd keep them balled up, not spread out.

As for his hair, he was wearing a ball cap with a San Francisco Giants logo on it into the restaurant. He would carefully remove it once he sat down and make sure his gray wig with a short pony tail was in place.

His glasses, with their thick lenses, would remain on. The oversized dark, brown, suede jacket would also remain on the entire time. It gave him a bulky look, adding girth to his midsection. The dark colored pants were nondescript. His black, dull shoes would not create any memories if someone was asked later what he was wearing.

One fixture he wanted people to remember was the dark brown cane. He planned to use it when entering the restaurant and then lean it up against his chair, prominently displaying it.

Last, but not least, he would carry a small, dark satchel.

When he was finished assembling everything, he looked critically at himself in the mirror, applied some more make-up, changed his contact lenses to make his dark brown eyes appear more of a dark green, and attached the fake mustache and bushy eyebrows.

"There. I'm ready to go." He looked at his oversized watch. "Time to head to the restaurant. I want to be there at least an hour ahead."

# Thirty-Two

**MARTA AND CLARK** were also dressing for the meeting. Clark's dark suit, watch, diamond cuff links, and ring on his pinkie finger looked expensive. He could easily pass for a well-dressed businessman. With his hair cut short, he could also pass for a no-nonsense type. For this meeting, he was not going to be chatty, but gruff and short in his responses; all business.

He and Ian had decided Marta should wear one of the bracelets Sami sent to Karla. They had been inspected and were definitely from the Paris heist. They figured if this man was involved in that, and if he saw it on Marta, he might make a mistake or slip up. Marta had her misgivings.

"I mean, yes, I want to wear it. Who wouldn't? But, this thing is valuable. Beyond valuable. And, it's on my wrist. What if I lose it? Are you nuts? Am I nuts?"

Her protests fell on deaf ears. Ian was insistent. "Don't worry, Marta. We have more agents in that restaurant than regular customers. Nothing is going to happen to it."

For that reason, Marta was to wear a sleeveless dress with a deep V neck and a shawl. The shawl would cover her wrists when she first sat down. At her neck, she would have a spectacular blue diamond pendant; one left to her by her grandma. The idea was for the man to notice this before she removed her shawl. She would have to decide when and how to reveal the bracelet. They would both watch for recognition on his face when she did.

Clark would take the lead, and Marta would react from his clues. They knew they were to leave the restaurant ahead of him, but didn't know what else he had planned or even if he had the diamonds with him. A lot of this was up in the air.

With a half hour to go, they walked outside to the waiting car. Their driver was another detective on the task force. "Well, guys. Showtime."

Marta and Clark nodded as Clark turned toward Marta. "It's not too late to back out. I don't want you to get hurt in case something goes wrong. Okay?"

She smiled. "I'm fine, and I want to do this. After all, I am all dressed up and have this sweet little bauble on my wrist. It would be shame to go back in the house and order pizza." She turned the bracelet so the light reflected off the diamonds, sending bight prisms of sparkles everywhere. "I suppose I have to give it back to Ian when we're done, huh?"

Clark smiled and nodded as he helped her into the car.

# Thirty-Three

**AT THE RESTAURANT,** Douglas posing as a waiter and George as a sommelier, were working with the real wait staff. The staff only knew they were there to scout their restaurant as a possible site for an upcoming film. Douglas and George had arrived at the same time as the rest of the staff.

They knew the appointed meeting time with Mr. Johanssen was for 6:30. Detectives Karla and Scotty, posing as tourists, had reservations at 6:15 and Roger from Interpol had a reservation at 6:00. Officers Stu Blenderman and Angie Wolf, posing as friends getting together for a drink after work, would arrive around 6:15. They would scan the restaurant, like they were looking for a place to sit. Charles from the FBI would be at the bar, nursing a beer.

Clark and Marta did not have a reservation. They were to tell the maître d they were meeting a gentleman, but did not know what he looked like. Hopefully Gustav, or whoever was meeting them, had informed him someone would be asking for him. They knew he was expecting only one man, not a couple.

At exactly 5:30 an elderly, somewhat portly, stooped-over, man entered the restaurant. Walking slowly with a cane, he carried a small satchel close to his left side. After speaking to the maître d, he was led to a table at the rear of the restaurant. He sat with his back to the wall, in a spot where he had access to watch most of the diners and the rest of the place.

Setting his satchel on the chair beside him, he picked up a menu and pretended to read it. He held it slightly lower than his face, so he could get a good look at all the diners and anyone entering the restaurant. As the waiter sat a glass of water in front of him, he told him he would wait to order until his guest arrived. Noticing Roger come in, he didn't like the looks of him at first. With his polished shoes and dark suit, he thought to himself that he would need to watch him. When Roger picked up the silverware and polished it with his napkin, Gustav relaxed. *Just a neat freak.*

Karla and Scotty entered, talking and laughing. They spent some time visiting with the maître d, who first took them to a table in the opposite part of the restaurant. Gustav couldn't hear the conversation, but they were then moved to a table towards the front. *Loud, obnoxious tourists.*

When Stu and Angie entered and looked around, Gustav didn't pay much attention to them. They were seated at a small table and declined a menu. Both were wearing business suits and both put their phones on the table.

A young Asian woman was seated in the corner opposite of him. He noticed her demure demeanor, but briefly glanced over her as she sat down and pulled out her phone. *Some people can't stay off their damned phones.*

Startling him, the sommelier came by to ask if he would like to know anything about the wine list. In a pronounced French accent, Gustav told him he was fine. *Hmm. He's new. I wonder where the old guy is.*

When two Chinese men, one young and the other one considerably older, entered and were seated several tables away from him, Gustav had a moment of panic. He immediately remembered Mr. Kim's latest message. *He said he knows where I go and what I do. Damn, I hope that's not him. I need to appease Mr. Kim with some of the other diamonds and then disappear. His latest text wasn't friendly. He could be a problem. A big one.*

Two more Asian men entered and sat along the far wall. *They're watching people, but they're trying to look like they aren't.*

*I wonder why and for whom. I need to stay vigilant. Not sure what Mr. Kim looks like as we've only dealt via courier before. But, I'm not worried about him recognizing me. Ever.*

He kept his eyes on the diners and the people at the bar. Nothing had created any red flags. Now, all he had to do was wait for Mr. Marsh. He knew what he looked like from the information he gathered on him. Supposedly, he was ruthless. That didn't bother Gustav. He also knew he wanted diamonds, any way he could get them. *What I've got should please him just fine.*

Pulling up his sleeve, he made a big deal of looking at his watch. Then, he carefully scanned the diners once more. The restaurant was filling up. Most of the ones he checked out were still here. It was now 6:30.

When the door opened and Mr. Marsh walked in, Gustav was upset. There was a woman with him.

# Thirty-Four

CLARK AND MARTA were shown to Gustav's table. Marta's arm with the bracelet was hidden under her shawl. She followed Clark to the table.

"Mr. Johanssen, I'm Mr. Marsh. No need to get up." Clark had seen the cane leaning against the table. He reached out to shake his hand, but Gustav didn't acknowledge the gesture. "I know you said to come alone, but Marie wouldn't let me out of her sight tonight. We've got a big evening planned. Don't we, dear?"

Marta smiled. "Yes, we do. My baby is going to buy me some diamonds. Right?"

Clark pulled out the chair for Marta, and they both sat across the table from Gustav, with their backs to the rest of the restaurant. Clark directly faced Gustav, with Marta to Clark's left. Marta's left arm was in her lap, the bracelet still hidden. When the sommelier and waiter stopped at their table, Clark ordered two glasses of wine and asked Gustav what he wanted.

Speaking softly, with a slight French accent, he declined anything to drink.

"Are you sure you don't want anything? I'm buying. We thought we'd stay for dinner. Want to join us?" Clark put his arm around Marta.

Gustav shook his head as he looked directly at Clark. "I'm here to do business. You got my instructions, and you've deliberately ignored them. Now, we can either do this transaction or not. What's it going to be?" His voice was soft, but the message was pure steel. He didn't acknowledge Marta.

Clark matched his demeanor. "Okay, old man. I want to see the diamonds. You're asking a pretty penny, and I don't even know what I'm getting. Maybe they aren't even what I want. Where are they?" His quiet words came across just as hard and cold. His hands rested on the table, as the waiter brought the glasses of wine and left.

Gustav reached into his satchel and brought out a small, black pouch. With one hand, he took a diamond from the pouch and laid it on top of the black fabric. The square cut, two carat stone glimmered in the candlelight. Marta inhaled and reached for the diamond with her right hand. "Not so fast." Gustav pulled it away from her. "Now, I need to see some money."

"That's a fine stone, but how do I know what else I'm getting? Where are the rest? I'm not about to hand you a bunch of money and have you rip me off. I need to see them or else we leave right now." Clark's message was clear.

Marta took the cue from Clark, gasped, let her shawl fall away from her arms, and brought her left arm onto the table. Reaching in front of her, she touched Clark's arm, fully exposing the brilliance of the bracelet. "But, you promised me some more diamonds. We can't leave now." Every magnificent stone in the bracelet caught all the light in the room, sending luminous, dancing sparkles to even the darkest corners, mesmerizing Gustav. Both Clark and Marta noticed his eyes widen, then harden. With the intake of his breath, his spine stiffened. All within one or two seconds. Then, just as quickly, he relaxed into his old man persona again. To a casual observer, nothing changed. But, to both Clark and Marta who were carefully watching him, it was noticeable.

Gustav's mind was working overtime. *She's wearing my bracelet. It's one of the bracelets Petrov stole from me. How'd they get it? Was Petrov working for this guy? How did she end up with it? This is troublesome.*

Almost immediately, he pulled his mind and eyes back to Mr. Marsh. "Okay. This is the way it works. You pay me a down payment; I give you this diamond. When I receive the rest of the money in my account, you'll be given an address where you can pick up the rest of the diamonds. That's the deal. Take it or leave it."

"Nope. Not gonna happen that way. How do I know you won't take the money and run? We need to do a trade. Pick a place, bring the stones, and I bring the money. Simple trade. That's MY deal. Take it or leave it."

Gustav figured the guy wouldn't like his first deal, so he had another one ready. He didn't want to be seen a second time by anyone. "Nope. Too big a chance of someone being there who shouldn't. Here's what I'm going to do. Your package of diamonds will be at the front desk of the Marriott Hotel at Fisherman's Wharf. You take that package and replace it with one with the money. Go there tomorrow morning at 9:00. I'll have someone watching to see you do it exactly like you should. If you try to cheat me, neither one of you will live to see the sun set. Got it?"

Clark seemed to be thinking about it. Deliberately, Marta moved her arm with the bracelet, creating more brilliance as the diamonds caught the light from the candle in the center of the table. Reaching across, she tugged at his arm. The bracelet practically danced by itself. "Please, honey. I really need a few more diamonds. A girl can never have too many. And, I'm tired of wearing the same ones all the time. Please . . . . ." More sparks lit up the entire area as the bracelet took on a life of its own. Its brilliance increased with every move she made.

Gustav tried not to look at the bracelet, but couldn't help himself. Inside, he was seething. *Damn. I've got to get it back. I must find out where this woman lives.*

Finally, Clark nodded, and smiled at Marta. "Okay. That will work. I'll be there."

Marta hugged Clark, giving him a kiss on the cheek. Her bracelet sparkled even more.

# Thirty-Five

**GUSTAV RELUCTANTLY TOOK** his eyes off the bracelet, put the diamond back in its pouch, and put it in his satchel. "Now, per our agreement, you need to leave. I can't take a chance you'll follow me. Or, else the deal's off."

"But, we were going to have dinner here and celebrate."

"Too bad. Find somewhere else. My business with you is done." *For now. I'll deal with the woman later and get my bracelet back.*

"Let's go, dear. We'll get the diamonds tomorrow." Marta and Clark stood up, Marta waved the bracelet around one more time as she thanked Gustav, and they left the restaurant. He fumed.

*Damn it. Damn that woman. She's history. That belongs to me. It's the one I told Mr. Kim he could buy. When I get it from her, I'll get him off my back.*

Sighing, he continued to sit, looking around at the remaining diners. No one seemed out of place, except for the guy at the bar. How long had he been there? *I seem to remember him being there quite a while. I'm going to watch him a few more minutes before I leave.*

When the guy drained his beer, paid the bartender, and left, Gustav felt relieved. He picked up his satchel and cane, and shuffled his way to the restroom. One of the reasons he picked this restaurant was that the restroom was located at the back, behind a small wall, totally out of view of any diners. It was also close to the kitchen and the back door. The day before, he had checked for cameras in the back alley and had found none.

Once inside the restroom, he locked the door, removed his glasses, wig, hat, and jacket. From his satchel he pulled out a thin windbreaker, 49er's cap, and dark glasses, and put them on. Over that, he placed a white chef's coat. He folded up his cane and stuffed it with everything else in his satchel, which he had unzipped to create a larger duffel bag. This took him less than three minutes.

Exiting the restroom, he stopped briefly to check out the restaurant. Nothing looked out of place. He made his way through the kitchen. This was prime dinner hour and everyone was busy. They didn't pay any attention to another prep cook walking through. In less than 30 seconds he was in the alley. The chef's coat came off and went in the duffle bag. His dark clothes blended into the darkening evening as he made his way to the bus stop.

# Thirty-Six

**BY THE TIME** Gustav left the restaurant, everyone else had played their part and was gone except for Douglas, George, and Roger. Roger had been working on his laptop, sitting in a corner where he could see just about everything that was going on. The one part he couldn't see was when Gustav went into the restroom, however.

But, George had. Unfortunately, though, the bartender had called to George just as he was watching the restroom door and he went to see what he needed. When he came back, the door was unlocked and the restroom was empty. Nothing. Quickly, he asked Douglas and the other waiters if they had seen the older man sitting at one of the back tables.

No one remembered when he left. Douglas had been busy at a table of older women who wanted to chat with him.

Then, he asked the maître d if he had seen him leave. Lastly, he went to Roger's table and asked him. Roger had seen Gustav at his table, but that was it. Neither had seen him walk out the front door. It was like the man disappeared into thin air.

"Is there a back door? That has to be how he left." Roger had gathered up his things, and they both went toward the kitchen. George asked the chefs and line cooks if they had seen an older man come through the kitchen on his way out the back. Nope. Nothing.

"He can't just disappear. We have to be missing something."

"Well, he's gone. Let's leave now and head to our meeting point. I'll clear it with the owner and see you there."

While everyone was gathering at Clark and Marta's to go over the evening, Gustav was entering his condo. He was not happy.

"Damn it. Where'd she get that bracelet? It wasn't a fake. It was the one from Paris; the one Petrov stole and supposedly gave to his stupid girlfriend. The one he told me he didn't have. Unless, this broad is a friend of the girlfriend and she gave it to her. Who is that broad, anyway? I need to see if I can find her. I have to have that bracelet. Mr. Kim would be appeased with at least one of them. But, maybe this broad has both of them. Maybe she has my ring. Wouldn't that be sweet?"

His mind was working overtime, his frustration building, confusion hampering his thoughts.

Finally, he replaced all his disguise items and looked through the file he had on Mr. Marsh. There was nothing about a girlfriend in it. His phone beeped with a text message. It was from Mr. Kim. He was upping the time frame. He wanted his diamonds in less than a week. The message ended with a threat.

Gustav paled when he read it.

# Thirty-Seven

**EVERYONE HAD MADE** it to their house from the restaurant, and Ian was conferenced in. "Thanks, Marta, for allowing us to meet here at your place."

"No problem. Since you all know Clark and I are engaged, this is his place, too."

"Okay. This is what we know for sure." They spent the next two hours going over every detail, no matter how minute. Everything about the man at the restaurant was dissected. Marta and Clark each gave an account of his face and eyes when he spotted Marta's bracelet.

"Marta did a wonderful job of flashing the bracelet. Needless to say, he was stunned initially to see that on her wrist. But, he recovered quickly. Then, each time she waved it around, I thought he was going to come across the table and grab it. Did you notice that, Marta?"

"Yeah. It's like his eyes had a laser beam to the bracelet. But, I thought it was kind of odd he didn't make any reference to it. I mean, if you have diamonds for sale, legit or not, wouldn't you at least say 'nice bracelet' or something? It was as if he didn't want us to see he noticed it. And, it was so obvious he noticed it. We would have had to be blind not to see how he reacted."

"I know. I also thought he might mention something about it, and was ready to tell him you needed another piece or two to keep you happy. And, you flashed it several times. Very well. Each time, he tried hard to ignore it. By now, he has to be wondering how and why you have it.

"To me, it tells me he knows about that piece. And, that tells us he is either Gustav or he was in on the heist with Gustav. Now, we just need to figure out how your sister ended up with it, Karla. And, we need to figure out about the rest of the pieces she sent to you."

The discussion continued. "Okay. Any other distinguishable features? What about his hands?"

"It was weird. His hands bothered me at first for their appearance."

"What do you mean?"

"Well, he kept them under the table most of the time. That's kind of unusual in itself. But, when he would place one on the table or when he put the pouch with the diamond on the table, his hand didn't fit with the rest of him."

Marta looked at Clark. "You saw his face up close. At first glance, he looked old. I didn't really want to stare at his face, but every time I looked at it, I swear he looked like he had on make-up. His face was too perfect. He had bushy, gray hair tied in a ponytail type thing, which could have been a wig. His eyebrows almost looked fake. I mean Halloween-ish fake. But, his hands, or what I could see of them, were much younger looking than his face. That's usually not right. Your hands typically age more quickly than your face. It's like they didn't match. And, why did he keep them hidden?"

"Were his hands unusually large?"

"Yeah, kind of. Again, it was hard to tell. I remember thinking it was odd that he always kept the hand which was on the table in kind of a fist. Like he didn't want us to see his whole hand. So, maybe they were larger than I realized."

"You're exactly right on all counts, Marta. His hands were always in a tight fist when we could see them, and they were large. He most definitely had on make-up. It was well done, however.

I'd have to say this is not the first time he's worn it. Also, he displayed his cane prominently. He wanted us to think he was old. That could also be why he didn't want to stand up or let us see him other than him slouching in his chair. George or Douglas, did you see him come in?"

George shook his head, but Douglas nodded. "Yeah, he kind of shuffled in and asked for the table at the back. When I watched him, my first thought was that he was acting. He just didn't look like a real older person. I can't put my finger on it, but there was something off about him. As for the table he reserved, he knew what he was doing. It was close to the restroom, too. It's just beyond me how he got out without any of us seeing him."

"Well, if his purpose was to fool you by being disguised as an older man, maybe he changed when he went to the restroom."

"Ian, that's possible. He had a small bag with him. The one where he pulled out the pouch with the diamond. But, he'd still have to walk out of the restaurant. Someone would have noticed."

"Was everyone in the restaurant questioned?"

"Yes, Karla, they were. No one had left their shift. And, no one was new. I'm thinking he didn't have an accomplice there. So, he had to slip out the back while the cook staff wasn't looking. That's the only thing that makes sense. We'll have to assume he changed clothes in the restroom. And, we'll have to assume he's not as old as he wanted us all to believe."

"Do you think he spotted any of us?"

Roger shook his head. "I really don't think so. I think he planned all of this, the disguise he wore in and the disguise he wore out. We're dealing with someone who knows exactly what he's doing. He had no reason to suspect any of us. The restaurant was busy, really crazy busy. And, that's exactly why he picked it and picked the time. Everything worked in his favor.

"Now, we just need to concentrate on the drop. As Clark said, he's leaving the diamonds at the front desk of the Marriott Hotel by Fisherman's Wharf. We can't assume he'll be the one doing this, and we don't how or who will come get the cash. He's already proven he's a master of disguises and misdirection. We'll have an agent at the desk, and she'll let us know when someone leaves the package.

"Ian, if it's okay with you, we need to proceed exactly like he told Clark to do. Clark, you should go to the front desk and ask for the package Mr. Johanssen left for Mr. Marsh. If the diamonds are there, take that envelope or package, and leave the envelope with the cash. Our agent will be the only other person there. We can't afford to spook him with any of us, in case he remembers us from the restaurant. He'll be watching people carefully."

"Roger, I agree. Clark, good luck. Let's all meet at the office tomorrow at 3:00. We should know more then. Have a good night, everyone."

After everybody left, Clark and Marta talked some more. Since Marta had a photo shoot the next morning, they decided it wasn't a good idea for her to go with Clark anyway. Since he was to be at the hotel at 9:00, posing as Mr. Marsh, they could meet back at the house before going to the meeting at 3:00.

# Thirty-Eight

**UNBEKNOWNST TO THE** group, Gustav had been to the hotel two days before he met with Clark and Marta. He figured the buyer, Mr. Marsh, wouldn't agree to the first deal, if he was anything like the other buyers. They never did. So, this was his back-up plan; the one he figured he would use.

When scoping out hotels, he picked one where tourists came and checked in at all hours. His ideal hotel had activities constantly happening, along with various conferences or meetings. There was less of a chance he would be remembered with so many people coming and going.

Not that it would do them any good. His disguise would be good. Very good.

The day he left his package, Gustav was dressed as a woman. Blond wig, plenty of make-up, padded bra, gray pantsuit, pointed toe, patent leather shoes, and a gray Coach handbag comprised his disguise. He waited until there were several other women at the Concierge desk, apologized as he reached in front of one woman, and handed the envelope to the Concierge. "Since I'm leaving town, a friend will come pick this up." She made a note, smiled at Gustav, and paid no attention to his southern drawl or elaborate outfit. When another woman interrupted, the Concierge promptly forgot about the one in the gray pantsuit.

Gustav exited the hotel, and caught a cab to take him to an apartment complex a block from where his condo building was located.

Now, today, the day Marsh was to pick up the envelope, he was sitting in a dark sedan with a good view of the front of the hotel. This time, he was a dark-haired woman in a pale pink jacket and gray pants. The gray bag had been replaced with a dark pink one, he wore dark glasses, and dark flats. He wore a disguise in case anyone happened to see him. Last night he put an 'Out of Order' sign on one of the meters just down the street to make sure he had a parking place where he could watch the front entrance of the hotel. His car windows were tinted just enough so no one could easily see him.

He knew Mr. Marsh would come for the diamonds. He could see he wanted them when he looked at his eyes last night. He also knew the woman with him had expensive tastes. He desperately needed that bracelet she was wearing. Mr. Kim was getting more impatient by the hour.

He sat in his car and watched the morning tourists. Shortly before 9:00 he saw Mr. Marsh exit a cab and enter the hotel. He had a briefcase with him. After about 10 minutes, he came back out of the hotel and left on foot. Gustav watched to see if anyone followed him, either in or out of the hotel. Seeing no one, he waited until Marsh was at the end of the block, and then he drove away, satisfied the plan was going according to schedule.

He would go back tomorrow when the lobby was full of people for the travel conference.

# Thirty-Nine

**INSIDE THE HOTEL** two SFPD detectives were at the front desk. To anyone watching, they appeared to be in training. They watched everything and every person who entered.

Clark did exactly like he was instructed by Mr. Johanssen. The envelope was retrieved from the front desk, and he left the one with the money. Exiting the hotel, he walked down the street. Detective Scotty Smith was discretely tailing him, making sure he was not followed. He noticed cars, including the one driven by Gustav, but did not react as there was a woman driving it.

When Clark made it to the appointed restaurant, Scotty followed and sat a different table. They both watched the door and the street. When Clark decided it was clear, he took a cab back to Marta's.

Gustav was at his condo by then, disguise put away, as he started to work on the next plan. His phone beeped with yet another text from Mr. Kim, with more dire consequences listed if Gustav didn't provide the bracelet. Quickly. He had to figure out a way to find that bracelet the woman was wearing. He was positive it was the one Mr. Kim wanted. He had never seen a bracelet sparkle like that one.

His hope was that she had his ring, too. Everything depended on that ring.

First, he paced. He always thought better when he was walking. He knew Petrov stole it from him, and he knew Petrov's girlfriend wore it to the party. But, when he questioned her on the yacht, she acted like she gave it back. "Somehow I believe her when she said she didn't have the bracelet or any of the diamonds. She didn't really look guilty. But, how did the woman with Marsh end up with one of the bracelets? Is she somehow connected to the model? If so, how? Is she from the modeling agency? Maybe I'll see her on their site."

Sitting down at his computer, he brought up the modeling agency's site and scrolled through pages of photos. Then he moved to their social media sites. Nothing about the woman he was looking for. "Damn. Who is she? And, why does she have my bracelet?"

"I need to pick up the money Marsh left. Let's see when the most people will be at the hotel." The first time he was there, he had picked up a brochure about upcoming events at the hotel. Tomorrow, a two-day travel conference was starting at 10:00. There would be lots of people registering for it in the morning and others registering to stay at the hotel. He would dress like a tourist and watch for an ideal time to pick up the envelope of cash.

He went into his disguise room to figure out what he was going to wear. As he pulled out shirts, something was bothering him. It was the brochure from the hotel. An image on it had puzzled him. He went back to the living room and grabbed the brochure. Scrutinizing it, he saw the image which was disturbing him. "It's HER. Damn it, it's her."

# Forty

ROGER HAD TAKEN all the security tapes from the hotel for the last few days and the task force was going through them, frame by frame. Everyone was looking first for an older man even though they knew he was probably disguised.

"Nothing. No one dropped off anything today. Yet, the envelope for Mr. Marsh was there. What's going on? Is anybody seeing anything that I'm not? I think we need to start fresh on this in an hour. Let's switch gears. What have we heard back from SFPD on the murder in Karla's sister's apartment?" He looked at George.

"Not much, unfortunately. We've learned more about the victim, however. His real name is Petrov Smit, and, like you know, he has been busted for theft, but he went by Peter Smith at the modeling agency here. He was a freelance photographer for them, but they didn't consider him the best, by any means. Apparently, Sami initially liked him, and that's why he could get her famous smile. So, they often put the two of them together.

"Everyone we talked to at the agency said they could see he was using her. And, two people told us that Sami was finished letting him stay with her and mooch off her. She was going to tell him it was time to move on, according to both Betty and another model. I don't know if he knew that or not. Roger, you can fill the group in on Paris."

"Okay. Petrov definitely traveled to Paris several times with a passport and identity as Peter Smith. His latest trip coincides with the murder of Matilda, her nephew, and the heist there. We have footage of him at de Gaulle airport, both arriving and departing. He could be involved. However, there's one problem. He's not nearly tall enough to be the one in the footage from her front door. And, he has small hands. We ruled him out as the thief until we noticed something on the last day when a person goes into her mansion. As our techs took the tape apart, frame by frame, and in some cases pieces of each frame, they realized there were two people on the last day. They do a really good job of standing in tandem, so it looks like one person."

"Why didn't they just disable that camera?"

"Good question. And, one we've been asking ourselves. The only thing we can think of is, they didn't know if that footage went directly to the security company or not."

"I suppose. But it seems kind of risky."

"Yeah, Clark, you're right. But, we have no other explanation. Right now, that's what we're thinking.

"Anyway, back to the last day. It really looks like two people. If that's the case, Petrov could have been one of them. Maybe Gustav is the other one. They could have been in the heist together. If that's true, there might be a reason Gustav is the one who killed Petrov. Maybe they had a falling out; maybe Petrov grabbed some of the diamonds; maybe Sami knew he had them; maybe things went awry; maybe a lot of things. This could explain why and how Sami had the diamonds she sent to Karla.

"Now, we did catch a break on the murder of the nephew. He had some dirt under his fingernails. Turns out, it was skin. He must have scratched his murderer. DNA puts it as Petrov's. That doesn't prove he was involved at the mansion or with the theft of the diamonds. But, he had to be involved somehow in order to have those bracelets and earrings."

"I'm still wondering how and why he gave them to Sami. You guys have the tape and witnesses' accounts from the party. Was that only one day before she was killed? The time frames match with the date my mailman told me the package was mailed. But, it was mailed in Sausalito. What the hell was my sister doing there when she was supposed to meet me for lunch in San Francisco?

"And, why was she in the water? She didn't just fall overboard. Someone put her there."

"Another question, Karla. Why did she leave and go somewhere alone? For that matter, why did Petrov let her take the jewelry with her? Or, did he know she had it? Was he the one who ransacked her apartment or did his killer?"

Ian had rejoined the conversation. "Okay, let's table those questions for right now. Let's go over the hotel tapes one last time, and then we can get together tomorrow. Who's watching the hotel to see if Gustav comes for the envelope you dropped off, Clark?"

"The staff will alert the manager, who will alert us when someone comes in to get the envelope. They know it's important."

"Okay. Roll the tapes one more time. Let's see if we notice anything."

# $\mathcal{F}$orty-One

**KARLA, ALONG WITH** everyone else on the task force, watched the tape again. "Wait. Stop right there." She pointed to a group of women surrounding the Concierge desk. "Did we look at this desk before? I know we thought the envelope was given to the front desk, but look at the tall woman. Doesn't she have something in her hand?"

"The date on this one was earlier than we were concentrating on. This would have been two days before the meeting with you, Clark. Good catch, Karla. It looks like she took something out of her purse. Let's look at it again."

"That purse is a Coach. I know my purses, because Sami was a sucker for all purses, especially expensive ones. It's too bad the other women are blocking the view."

They all viewed this part one more time, in super slow motion. "I don't know now that I see it again. She's probably part of that group of women. They're all kind of gathered around the desk."

"No, Karla. It registered with you. We'll ask the staff if they know the group, what they were doing, and if they know how many were together. That woman is tall, taller than the rest. We know the thief in Paris was tall, around six foot, three inches. We also believe Gustav to be shorter based on what we saw in the restaurant. But, if he's using disguises, maybe he's trying to make us think he's shorter than he is.

"So, based on that, let's have our guys at the hotel keep their eyes out for a tall woman. She might be the one who comes to pick up the envelope. She could even be an accomplice of Gustav.

"Now, let's call it a day. You all have copies of this tape. Watch it, dissect it, and jot down anything you think is important. Nothing should be overlooked. See everyone back here tomorrow."

# Forty-Two

**GUSTAV WAS LOOKING** at the brochure from the hotel. On it were pictures of last year's conference, and Marta's photo was right in front of him. "This is fantastic."

With renewed energy, he spent the next hour Googling her, her travel consultant company, and every little detail he could get his hands on. The one thing he couldn't find was her address. "I wonder why she's involved with Mr. Marsh. I wonder if he knows she isn't just a socialite. Maybe she truly is a friend of that model. That would be fantastic if she had all my jewelry. Now, how do I find her?"

Picking up the brochure, he looked at it again and discovered what he had missed the first time. She was speaking at the conference tomorrow at noon.

"Even better. I'll head to the hotel, hang around until she's finished speaking, and follow her when she leaves. She'll lead me right to her home. This is getting easier and easier. I can snag the bracelet, and see if she has the rest of the diamonds. I'll bet she has my ring. If not, she will tell me where it is."

He smiled at the thought of the ring. "The ring. Oh, that ring. I can just see it. My future is in that ring.

"I'll be able to get that sadistic Mr. Kim off my back, pick up my money from the hotel, and get the hell out of town. I've been

107

hearing about some emeralds in Cozumel. Some rich dude took them out of Venezuela or Brazil or somewhere and has them hidden in a hotel safe. Ha! Not safe after I get there.

"First things, first. The bracelet."

Entering his disguise room, he laid out what he was going to wear tomorrow. Contemplating how he was going to be dressed when he watched her, he decided he needed two different disguises. "I'd bet she won't be wearing the bracelet to speak to a bunch of travelers. That means I have to get her to hand them over to me, and I don't want her to know what I look like. Hmm. Have to think about this a little more."

# Forty-Three

**AS GUSTAV WAS** planning and plotting how to get the bracelet, Mr. Kim paced in his hotel suite. This was becoming a fiasco. He couldn't believe Gustav kept putting him off. That meant only one thing. Gustav didn't have the bracelet. He thought about killing him, but he really needed that bracelet. It meant the world to his father.

Mr. Kim knew about the back-stabbing, slimy Petrov, and figured he played into this somehow. But, according to his sources, he knew Petrov was dead. He didn't know who killed him, but figured it was probably Gustav. He knew how that man worked. He always got rid of his accomplices. Always. That was something he admired about him.

So, did Petrov steal the bracelet, and Gustav had to kill him? Or, did Petrov already sell the bracelet out from under Gustav's nose? Something wasn't quite adding up.

He had been to the same party as Petrov and his girlfriend, and saw the bracelet on her wrist. He knew it was THE bracelet, but didn't know who she was or why she would be wearing it. Was Gustav there, too? He hadn't seen her speak to anyone for any length of time. And, he really didn't know what Gustav looked like. Yet. His informants were working on that.

He also spotted the theft of the diamond bangle from the old lady Petrov had schmoozed and even saw the cop watch them.

But, like the cop, he missed Petrov and the girl leave. Too bad.

Maybe, if he could find the girl, he'd have some info on Petrov. Maybe that would lead him to Gustav. Right now, his speculations were wasting time, and that didn't set well in his super-controlled world. "I need to stay on him. I need my informant to give me his best description of him. Time to move on this one. Father will be pleased once we get that bracelet. Then he can rest."

He would up the pressure, have his informant find him, follow him, and deliver a serious message. It was time to be finished with this guy.

Turning on his television to a local news station, he paced, letting the background noise help him think. Not really noticing anything as he was deep in thought, he looked up when an image caught his eye. It looked like the girl from the party; the one with Petrov. He stopped and turned up the volume.

The reporter was telling about how and where she was found. The police had no leads about her death and were asking for anyone with information about her to come forward. There was a substantial reward. "So, she's dead. Did Gustav or Petrov kill her? Why?" He spoke to no one in particular, and continued to watch as they detailed the girl's career. "Huh. A model." They gave the agency name, reiterated the reward, and moved on to another story. He turned the volume down.

"I wonder. What did the model do with the bracelet? I could see either Petrov or Gustav killing her to get the bracelet. But, if Gustav has it, why is he giving me the run-around. Has he sold it more than once? Or, does he really not have it? That means Petrov had it, gave it to the girl, and Gustav doesn't know where it is. Did she have it on her when she drowned?"

# Forty-Four

**THE FOLLOWING MORNING,** Marta and Clark were going over their plans for the day. Marta was heading to the hotel to speak at noon and would be home around 4:00. Clark was meeting with some of the detectives as they worked through the death of Sami and Petrov. Then, he was going with Karla to Sami's apartment to oversee the clean-up of it.

"I'll see you back here after 6:00 or so. Okay?"

"I'll stop and get stuff for dinner after my talk. I always have lots of people asking questions, so that will be about the time I get home, too. How's Karla doing, do you think?"

"She's tough, but this hit her hard. Sami was her only family, and I think Karla felt responsible for her. I'm hoping today she can get some closure. It's going to be a rough day for her."

"She's set a date for a private funeral service, which we're invited to. Then, after all the rest of this mess is cleaned up, she's going to have a celebration of Sami's life. She says it's what Sami would have wanted. I just hope that happens sooner rather than later."

"Yeah, me, too. Why don't you tell her we can host the celebration here? We have the room and then she wouldn't have to worry about finding someplace."

"Good idea. Thanks. I'll let her know and find out what date she's thinking about."

Marta nodded and smiled, packed up her bag of information for her talk, and gave Shadow a pat on the head. When she stood up, Clark kissed her, and they both left the house.

At the same time, Gustav left his condo. Dressed as a business man, he wore a dark suit, white shirt, red tie, dark shoes and a dark black wig. His make-up gave him a Hispanic look. Even his hands fit the skin tone, thanks to the self-tanning lotion he used. He would make sure Marta was speaking at the appointed time, and then follow her when she left.

He settled in to wait. He had once again parked his car across the street. This time, it was about a block away. His second disguise was waiting in his bag in the van.

# Forty-Five

ABOUT 3:00 MARTA exited the hotel's parking ramp. Gustav knew it was her as she drove right past him.

He followed her to the grocery store and then to a house in Pacific Heights, hanging back so she wouldn't notice him. Traffic wasn't heavy, but he could easily lose himself with the rest of the cars. When a garage door went up, she drove into the garage, and the door shut. He kept on going. Luckily, his delivery van was parked only about 10 minutes away.

He drove to it, changed clothes, and drove the van back to her house. When she answered the doorbell, he held out his small tablet device. An envelope was tucked under his arm. "I have a special delivery for a Mr. Swenson." He had found her real name to be Marta Swenson, and he wanted to check about a Mr. Swenson. Was the man he knew as Mr. Marsh really her boyfriend or was something else going on? He was hoping no Mr. Swenson lived here. If he did, he had an envelope ready.

Marta looked at him, drying her hands on a towel. It was obvious she was busy. That was good for him. "I'm sorry, there is no Mr. Swenson. Did you mean Mr. Moreno? He's not here right now."

"I'm sorry. The envelope says Mr. Swenson. I'll return it. Sorry to have bothered you, Ma'am." His accent had a deep-southern drawl, with just a hint of old Mexico. He tipped his hat and returned to his white, non-descript van.

When Marta shut the door, Shadow was standing about a foot behind her. Normally a peaceful, furry, long-haired Maine Coon cat, he was now twice his usual size. His fur stuck up everywhere, his tail was fluffed up like an overblown feather duster, his eyes were narrowed slits, and a menacing growl came from somewhere deep inside him. This was not a critter to be reckoned with.

"What the hell? What's the matter, Shadow?"

His growl continued as he looked past Marta to the now closed front door. Marta looked at the door, opened it a crack, and looked outside. Nothing.

"Shadow, there is nothing out there." Then, she had a thought. "Did you not like the delivery man?"

Shadow was slowly returning to the normally docile animal that he was. His growl stopped, and he walked toward the door, sniffing. "You didn't like him, did you?" She reached down to stroke his head and he purred. "Whew. You really got upset. I wonder why?"

# Forty-Six

**WHEN CLARK RETURNED** home, Marta relayed Shadow's reaction to the delivery man to him. "I've never seen him so upset and riled up. The fur was impressive, but his growl was scary." Shadow now lay purring in Marta's lap and closed his eyes when Clark rubbed his head.

"What did the guy look like? Did you notice anything unusual about him at all? Did you see what he was driving?"

"He drove a white van, but I have no idea if it had any logos on it. He parked it in the driveway, which is odd for a delivery service, now that I think about it. Let's see. He was a lot taller than me, he wore a dark blue shirt and pants, his name tag read Randy, I think. He also had on a dark blue cap and I saw no hair sticking out from it. Nothing unusual at all."

"Tell me again what he was trying to deliver."

"He had one of those hand-held reader things and he asked for Mr. Swenson. He said he had an envelope or a package for him. When I said there was no one here by that name, he thanked me and left. He was very polite; even called me Ma'am in a southern drawl."

"Okay. Now close your eyes and picture him. Did he, in any way, remind you of the man from the restaurant?"

Marta took a deep breath and closed her eyes. She shook her head and opened them. "No. Sorry. I really don't think so. He was a lot taller than him and I'd have to say, thinner. He almost appeared to be Latino. His face was quite dark, and his eyebrows were smooth, not bushy like that guy's."

"Okay. He may or may not be connected to Mr. Johanssen or to Gustav. I'm just suspicious of everything and everyone right now. And, it's awfully strange the way Shadow reacted. So, there was something he didn't like, but that doesn't necessarily mean it was Gustav. I'm going to ask SFPD to do extra drive by trips around here for a couple of days."

"Okay. So, tell me what you found out about Karla's sister's murder."

"Let's have a glass of wine, and I'll tell you what the detectives think."

# Forty-Seven

**TO SAY MR.** Kim liked things orderly was a huge understatement. He paid his informants well for quality work, and he demanded 110%. Always. This informant was worth what he paid him. It was of no importance to him to know how the man obtained his information, just to deliver correct information. Now, his informant had found Gustav and had given his condo's address to him.

After checking out the condo's website, he hacked into their records and checked out renters within the last year. He discovered a Mr. John Jay rented one and a Mr. Jay Johnson rented another, on the same day, using the same bank account. It looked like one rented via email and one in person, according to the records he pulled up. He was positive they were the same man and he was positive this man was Gustav. Positive. "Stupid man."

Further information his informant gave him had a better description of Gustav. Over six feet tall, a fairly muscular man, over 50 years old, with short, dark hair. He directed his informant to keep an eye on the building. It paid off.

Mr. Kim kept reading the report his informant just sent to him. A man, matching their description of Gustav, exited the building, drove to the Marriott where he stayed in his parked car for most of the day. At 3:15 he left, drove slowly through one neighborhood, and then stopped at a white van parked several blocks away. The driver of the car got into the van, and after a few minutes drove to a house in the Pacific Heights neighborhood, the same one he had just driven past.

The driver went to the door, stayed only a couple of minutes, then drove back to where he left his car. The van stayed parked on the street. The man drove to the condo building.

The informant also gave Mr. Kim the address of the home where Gustav went.

Checking addresses and property records, Mr. Kim discovered the home belonged to a Marta Swenson. He then delved into her life and discovered she was a travel consultant and photographer. When he saw a photo of her, he remembered seeing her before.

It wasn't long before he remembered exactly when and where. She and another man had met an older gentleman at the restaurant the other night. Mr. Kim always made it his business to watch other people when he was in a public space. Paranoid to a fault, he knew several things about people at the restaurant. There was an undercover cop sitting at a table by himself. He had seen his type before and knew exactly what to look for. And, he'd bet a lot of money the sommelier was undercover as well. More than once, his life depended on observing things like this.

What were they doing there? They didn't appear to be watching anybody, but he couldn't afford to make assumptions. He figured somewhere, someone was always watching him.

Thinking of the woman, he scanned her travel site, looking for photos of the man she was with. Trying to remember exactly what her companion and the older man looked like, he drew sketches on a piece of paper. Her companion had his back to him. All he could come up with was that he was tall and well dressed. Could that have been Gustav? He didn't think this man was quite in his 50s, but the rest of the description could fit.

The older man at the table was quite hunched over and seemed to take up a lot of space. At the time, the thought that went through his mind was that the guy was trying too hard to look old and hunched. Maybe it was a disguise. But, why? Could that have been Gustav? Was he disguised? But, again, why?

The profile his informant gave him didn't completely fit either of the men at that table. Yet, this woman was with both of them and then followed by Gustav today.

Something was missing. Or, he was missing something important. But, what? Did it have to do with the woman? He'd tell his informant to keep watching Gustav. He wanted that bracelet in the next few days. He'd give Gustav a new deadline.

He sent him another text message.

# Forty-Eight

CLARK FILLED MARTA in on what the police knew for sure about Sami's murder, the envelope she sent to Karla, and her apartment.

"The M.E. has given us an approximate date of her death. This is what we know. She went to the party on Nob Hill and went home with the now-dead photographer, Petrov, the same day. This was verified by the security tapes and by the guard at her apartment building because, the next morning Petrov left and came back with coffee. He talked to the guard briefly. We've got the tapes and the guard's accounting of this.

"Shortly after that, Sami leaves, telling the guard she is going to a party on a yacht. She's excited. About an hour later, Petrov comes down and asks the guard if Sami left the building while he was getting coffee. The guard tells him no, thinking it was kind of an odd question at the time.

"Now, this is something the guard mentioned to the detectives. He hadn't thought too much about it at the time. Apparently, a fire marshal called him and told him there would be a routine inspection. Sure enough, a guy dressed like a fire marshal comes, talks to the guard a few minutes, goes in the building, and is there about an hour. This happened on the day we think Petrov was killed.

"In talking to the SFFD, there was no routine inspection scheduled for that building on that date. The apartment building's security cameras don't get a good view of the guy, either. He was dressed in a Fire Captain's uniform, smart enough to spot the cameras, and stay away from their direct view, even in the elevators.

"Was this Gustav? It could be. From the guard's description, he was a tall guy with broad shoulders. He didn't remember his hands."

Marta had been listening and nodding. "This is good. Right?"

"Right. Now, using the guard's explanation of a party on a yacht and the fact that Sami mailed Karla an envelope from Sausalito, SFPD canvassed the marinas there. First, they went to a boat rental place to inquire about a large boat or yacht that had been recently rented. If they found nothing, they were going to check out private yachts. This rental place did have a large boat which was rented on the right day, but, the renter doesn't fit the description of Gustav.

"When they checked the log, they discovered the person who rented that particular boat was an older French guy who used a passport for identification. They have a copy of it and Interpol is running that. The employee who worked that day was called in and asked about this renter. He sort of remembered an old guy renting a big boat. When asked to describe him, he just said old and tall."

"Not much help, huh?"

"But, it gets better. The young guy definitely remembered this old guy having a hot chick with him. Those are his words. So, the detectives showed him a photo of Sami. And, guess what? She was with him."

"Sweet. I mean, it's good to find out more. Right?"

"Yeah. Apparently, they arrived separately. But he did get a good look at her."

"So, was she there when he returned the yacht?"

"That's where the young man gets a little fuzzy. He doesn't remember. He thinks he would have remembered seeing her again, but it was a busy day and he couldn't be sure. For all he knows, the old guy already had helped her off when he came in to sign the paperwork. He feels bad, but he just doesn't know. SFPD is checking over the yacht with special equipment now. They're looking for anything out of the ordinary on that particular yacht. Maybe they'll get lucky and find Sami's hair or something.

"Next, the detectives went to the post office in Sausalito, as that was the postmark on the envelope she sent to Karla. Their security cameras have her mailing an envelope in the lobby. She picks out an envelope, takes some things out of her purse, puts them in, and seals it up. We're assuming it was the jewelry and the note. Then, she goes to the stamp machine, buys stamps, puts them on, and puts the envelope in the mailbox. She doesn't talk to anyone, and it doesn't look like she is with anyone else. She appears to be in a hurry. And, the time frame is just before the old guy rents the yacht."

"So close and yet, nothing definite."

"I brought home some photos the detectives are using. There are a couple of the yacht from the marina in Sausalito and the rest from the beach where she was found. She had been in the water a little while, but they could tell she was wearing a dress. She had on one shoe, one costume jewelry ring, and nothing else that really helps. She was caught in some beach towel. They're not sure if the towel was already there and she just got caught in it or how it is related.

"According to the M.E., she died of a puncture wound to her neck and bled out before she entered the water. So, somebody killed her and tossed her in the water. No positive identification of where or who, but everything points to Gustav. Especially if he was the boat renter." Clark took the photos out of an envelope and handed them to Marta. "I know you've seen ones of people who have died, but a couple of these aren't very nice."

Marta nodded, took a sip of wine, and took the photos. Choking on her wine, she sputtered. "I know this towel. How do I know this towel?" Laying it aside, she looked at another photo. "This boat." She looked at Clark.

"Wait here."

# Forty-Nine

MARTA GRABBED HER laptop from her office,
opened the files of photos, and scanned to the file she had saved to
show Clark. "I almost forgot about these. I was going to show them
to you in hopes the Coast Guard or somebody could enhance it
and fine this guy for dumping his trash in the ocean.

"But, look. Isn't that the same towel? And, the boat. It looks
like that boat. Right?"

Clark scanned through her photos, then enlarged the one
with the best view of the towel. He compared it to the photo he
brought with him. Then, he did the same with the best shot of the
yacht. "The yacht is definitely the same. Look at these markings. I
wouldn't think there is more than one like this at that Marina. The
numbers are hard to see. Maybe a different program would make
them appear clearer. I'm sure you've tried everything."

"Yeah. But, I don't have big, expensive photo programs. At
the time, it wasn't as if he was directly in my sight but I tried to get
anything that might cause him to get a fine. I was concerned about
the garbage he was throwing in the ocean. Do you think the police
or FBI would have a better enhancing program? And, what about
the towel? Doesn't it look like this one?"

"It does. But, that might be a common towel pattern. I'll have
to see if it's enough of a match. Let's say it all matches. We still

don't have a good description of the man who rented the yacht. An old guy doesn't narrow it down for us. All we know is Sami was onboard with the renter, after she went to the post office.

"Was she concerned about this guy? Or, was she concerned about the man in her apartment? It had to be one of those. Karla said it wasn't like to her to mail something to her. She said Sami was smart but not exactly street smart. She was too nice and believed everyone else was, too."

"Yet, something about these pieces of jewelry bothered her."

"I know. Now, with these photos, we have more of the puzzle. I'm going to send them to Ian to have Interpol take a look and to George at SFPD, who can give them to his chief. I'll send them on to Roger as well. Somebody might be able to get a cleaner look." He emailed the file to all of them as they talked through the case.

"They are still missing the ring she talked about in the note. It might be the big one mentioned in the description from the Paris police. If that's the case, it's a spectacular piece. So, where is it? Sami must have seen some spectacular ring in order to mention it. And, she must have been impressed by it, but, she didn't wear it to the party the day before she was killed and she didn't send it to Karla. That means she hid it somewhere or wore it when she went on the boat. Karla thinks she probably had it on her somewhere, either wearing it or in her purse."

"Did SFPD go through her apartment?"

"Yeah. Thoroughly. Karla even went through it carefully and found nothing hidden where she thought Sami might have put it. More than likely, the ring is now at the bottom of the ocean.

"On to another disturbing situation. I think I mentioned Ian has intel that puts Mr. Kim, the sadistic gem buyer, here in San Francisco. He's been spotted by one of Ian's best operatives, who knows how to watch characters like Mr. Kim.

"He's been seen in a couple of different spots. Guess where one of them was."

Marta shook her head and looked at Clark. "I have no idea."

"At the restaurant the night we were there."

"What? Why was he there? Coincidence?"

"He shows up in some surveillance footage of the people at the restaurant. A much older, Chinese man and he are having dinner. It could be just that . . . dinner. But, knowing what we do now, I have my doubts."

"Who's the other man?"

"That's just it. He's a ghost. We can't find anything on him. He doesn't show up in any files. Anywhere. No facial recognition appears anywhere. Nothing. It's like he doesn't exist."

"But, if he was a normal, law abiding citizen, why would there be anything on him?"

"A couple of things are causing red flags. First, he's with Mr. Kim. That's bad news by itself. Second, he doesn't have a driver's license, a voting record, doesn't own property or pay taxes, and no IRS record. Nothing at all. Even law abiding citizens have some piece of identification and pay taxes. Not him. Which means he's probably not US. But, Interpol has nothing on him, either."

"How about a passport?"

"Nope."

"I don't suppose you have his fingerprints?"

"No such luck. Looking at the tape, he doesn't touch the menu. He does touch the glasses and silverware, but they were put through the dishwasher. We had no reason to ask the restaurant to hold those from the other tables."

"Did you hold them from our table?"

"Yes. The only thing Mr. Johanssen touched was the menu. And, it disappeared. He must have taken it with him. We don't really see that on the tape because he was sitting in the darkest corner. He knew what he was doing the whole time."

"So, what's the next step? Do you follow Mr. Kim? I know you have some more of the diamonds, the ones you picked up at the hotel. What about the rest? Aren't there quite a few missing still?"

"Yes, on all questions. We follow Mr. Kim, at least as best we can. He's slippery. And, yes, there are a lot still missing."

"What about the guy who's a ghost?"

"Ian is working on him."

Clark took Marta's hand as he pulled her toward him. "Okay, enough for one night. What do you say we head upstairs? I can think of better ways to end the evening."

# Fifty

**GUSTAV WAS LOOKING** for an opportunity. He didn't necessarily want to kill the woman; he just wanted his diamonds. And, he knew she had a least one of the bracelets. With any luck, she had everything. He could do a quick entry, grab his jewels, and be long gone before she knew they were missing. He was good at this type of thing. She'd never know he was even there.

The next morning, he parked down the street and was watching her house with binoculars. This time he was posing as a salesman for a security company. He figured he'd have to keep tabs on her house for a few days before he could go in. Instead, he got lucky. Early in the morning one car left her house. He waited a while and a second car left. "Mr. Marsh must be staying with her. Good thing I waited."

Parking his car a few houses away, he scanned the neighborhood before he got out. He didn't see the other car and its occupant, watching him from afar.

Gustav's white, short-sleeved shirt and dark blue pants appeared professional and his hat had a company's logo. The clipboard and brochures were in an official looking briefcase. With his make-up, glasses, and hat, he looked like an older man with no distinguishable features. He could have been anyone. The first time he was at her door, he had noticed a security camera. He'd avoid it as best he could this time. Even if she looked at the footage, she'd see nothing that gave her a good look at him.

He had his speech rehearsed, in case there was still someone home.

At her front door, he kept his head down as he rang the doorbell. Just to be certain, he rang it again. Then knocked. Hearing no one respond, he first picked the lock, and then worked his way through her alarm system. "Damn. This is a good one. I hope I got it all." Listening for a secondary sound to indicate a problem, nothing beeped. He figured he was okay. Once inside, he hurried up the stairs, assuming her bedroom was on the second floor and that would be where she kept her jewelry. "Aha. Found a jewelry box. Right where it should be." Rummaging through it, he found nice pieces. But, not the ones he wanted. "Damn it. This can't be. Where would she put it?"

Quickly, he searched the rest of the bedroom, looking for another jewelry box, as sirens blared off in the distance. Nothing was obvious to him. He looked for pictures on the wall which could be a front for a wall safe. Still nothing. Frustrated, he looked around, mumbling. "What am I missing?"

Just then, a deep growl came from somewhere above him. He was being watched. The watcher was not a happy cat. The growl intensified.

Those sirens appeared to be coming closer and that bothered him almost as much as the growl. He headed toward the bedroom door, just as the growl deepened. Shadow lunged down off the top of a tall dresser and made a swipe, claws out, connecting with his bare arm. Making a weak attempt to swat at the cat, he knew he had to get out of there quickly.

Running down the stairs and out the front door, he slowed to a fast walk as he made his way to his car. Yes, those sirens were getting closer. Jumping in, removing his wig and hat, he tossed them under a blanket on the floor and donned another set.

Slowly, he pulled away from the curb. Now, he was just an old lady with long, bleached blonde hair, a large pink hat, and granny glasses. The police car went right by him and stopped at the house he just left.

"Too close. That alarm must have had another level I didn't catch."

Mad at himself for not noticing the extra alarm, and mad at her for not having the diamonds, he grumbled all the way to his condo. His arm began to hurt where the cat's claws had connected. Blood was slowly dripping down his arm.

"Okay. Plan B. She's gonna tell me where they are."

# Fifty-One

CLARK AND MARTA separately received calls from the alarm company, asking for their passwords. When told there was a breach on the alarm, both of them rushed home. One policeman was at the front door, waiting. Clark and he entered the house and searched through the rooms. When they were finished, Marta entered and discovered an upset Shadow.

She picked him up, to calm him down. "Someone was here."

"Are you sure? We didn't find anything right off, but you'll want to look around." Marta nodded to the officer.

"How do you know someone was here? Is it Shadow?"

"Yeah. He's upset. Really upset. And, that's not like him. Unless he doesn't like someone, he's always friendly. Look at him. He's shedding like crazy, and he's pacing. Something really bothered him."

The police officer bent down, and scratched Shadow behind his ears. "He is a friendly one." He stood up. "Can you take a few minutes to see if anything was disturbed? You can always look later, but let's see if anything is obvious." His partner had been dusting for fingerprints.

Marta made a quick look at the downstairs. "I really don't have lots of valuable things here. This one painting is probably the most expensive piece here and it seems to be okay. Let me look in my office at my computer and cameras. Those would be something that might interest a thief." After a quick look there, she came back out. "Nothing has even been moved."

"How about jewelry?"

Marta, Clark, and the officer went upstairs, into the bedroom. Her jewelry box was closed and sitting right where it should be. But, when she opened it, she found things all messed up. "Okay. Someone was here, and messed up my jewelry. Things are not in the spots where I put them."

"Can you tell if anything was taken?"

"The most valuable pieces I have are from my grandma, and I keep them locked up. My other most valuable piece is my engagement ring from Clark and I wear it. The rest are real but not valuable enough to steal. And, anyway, they all seem to be here."

"Wait a minute. Clark, you don't suppose . . ."

"Yes, I do."

"Damn."

The officer looked from Marta to Clark. "Want to tell me what's going on?"

Clark nodded. "We are both involved in a task force focusing on some stolen diamonds from Paris. You'll have to ask your supervisor to fill you in. All I can tell you is that Marta wore one of the stolen pieces as part of our task force. I'm thinking, and probably so is Marta, the guy we met was the one who broke in here. He was looking for that piece."

"I am thinking exactly that. And, it bothers me. A lot. How does he know who I am? How does he know where I live? What the hell is going on?"

Shadow meowed. As Marta bent down to pick him up, she noticed the white fur on his front right paw was tinged pink. "Clark. Look. Is this blood?"

# Fifty-Two

ONCE BACK AT his condo, Gustav swore. Then, he paced. And, swore some more. "They're mine, and she has them. I know she does. Maybe there was a safe, and I missed it. I can't risk going back. There'll be cops all over now."

The back of his arm stung where Shadow's claws had scratched him. Looking at it, he saw more dried blood covering the mark. "Damn cat." After wiping it clean again, he sat down, his head in his hands. "How the hell am I going to get those diamonds? Do I grab her?" His mind worked overtime. Every plan he came up with wasn't workable.

"Back to square one. What do I know about the woman, Marta?" Meticulously working through everything he remembered from the night at the restaurant, he devised a plan. His mind sorted out facts and questions. She liked diamonds or she wouldn't have been wearing his bracelet.

Marsh. It was obvious he doted on her. He'd bet a lot of money Marsh gave her the bracelet. But, where did he get it? Did he buy it from the model? Why would the model just give up the jewelry?

Or was the model a friend? "I can't see her just giving it to somebody. But, if she sold the diamonds, where's the money?"

His thoughts were jumbled and confusing. They went round and round in his mind.

Back to Marsh. He HAD to be the one with it. So, the model was a friend of his. Or, he paid her for it. Remembering how Marsh looked at her, he would bet a lot of money Mr. Marsh would do anything for her. That's when it hit him.

"He's the key. I'll make him believe she's in danger. That way, I can go back in, grab the diamonds, get Mr. Kim off my back, and get out of town. She has to have the ring. Where else would it be?

"If she dies in the process, no loss."

# Fifty-Three

CLARK AND MARTA had been talking and planning, too. Shadow's paw had been cleaned, the fur and claws clipped, and the samples sent to the lab, in hopes of getting any DNA from it. There wasn't a lot of fur or blood, but Clark had seen the lab do more with less.

Clark had already contacted the SFPD and asked for more police presence in the area. Once again, they looked at the front door security camera footage, and saw a person, probably a man by the size of him, hunched over and obviously avoiding the camera.

"Whoever broke in, knew the camera was there. We've got nothing usable from that one. I'm going to have another one installed with a different angle. Even though this was probably a one-time deal, it still wouldn't hurt to have more than one view.

"Now, we both need to be careful and extra-vigilant. Several things bother me. If this guy is desperate, he may come back. If this was Gustav and if he thinks you have the bracelet, he most likely will come back. That means the guy we met at the restaurant was somehow involved with the heist and is involved with Gustav.

"Whoever it is, he may be in over his head with Mr. Kim, his Chinese buyer. Ian is pretty sure he's heavily involved in this. He's probably the buyer for the bracelet." Clark hugged Marta.

"Ian also believes Gustav is not stupid, so, if it was him, he'll assume you are adding more police around here. And, I don't think he knows about me being here. Somehow, he'll try again, but it makes sense he'll try to get to you and the bracelet another way now. Not here. What's the rest of your week like? Where are you going? Are you anywhere alone?" They both sat down.

"I'm meeting with my website designer tomorrow at his office downtown. After that, I was going to work on my next tour to Venice. Remember, it's the one to my vineyards in the Veneto area? You were going to come along. Is that still the plan?"

"Absolutely. How long are we staying?"

"At least three weeks, if that's okay with your schedule."

"I've already told Ian we'll be in Venice. Now, you said you were going to work on that trip. Where are you doing that?"

"Here, in my office. I usually make a bunch of calls to people who have either signed up or expressed interest, and then set the meeting dates. I put together their final brochures and paper-work. Why?"

"Well, let's coordinate our schedules so you're not anywhere alone for a while. When you leave here, have the police follow you. Okay? My gut tells me Gustav wants that bracelet in a bad way, or he or his guy wouldn't have broken in here in the middle of the day. I'm beginning to think the man we met in the restaurant, Mr. Johanssen, is really Gustav. Everything points to him, and this break-in adds to my suspicions. I still have the phone we used to contact him, but I've had nothing from him since the restaurant."

"Has the money been picked up from the hotel?"

"Not yet, and that's another curious thing. He's apparently try-ing to out-wait us.

"I also need to check with Roger and George to see if they know any more about the rest of the stolen diamonds. I wonder if any of the rest have surfaced or if any other buyers, legit or not, have entered the playing field. And, we need to see if they were able to get any prints from the break-in here."

# Fifty-Four

MR. KIM HAD received another report from his informant. He was following Gustav and detailed his day for Mr. Kim. He was curious about the woman. "There seems to be a definite connection between the woman and Gustav. She's either in on all of this with him or he thinks she has something. Which is it?

"Time to put the screws to that man. I'm tired of waiting. We need to get out of here. Father is failing fast."

He sent a text to Gustav, telling him he had 72 hours to get the diamond bracelet and earrings to him. The threat he made, if that didn't happen, was real. He also made a reference to the situation at Marta's. "That will make him wonder. And, I hope he slips up." He turned to the older man sitting in the hotel suite.

The man nodded at Mr. Kim. "Yes. Have him dealt with just as soon as we get those diamonds. He has served his purpose, and we no longer need him. I will finally have what is mine."

Mr. Kim smiled and bowed his head.

# Fifty-Five

**AT SAMI'S APARTMENT,** Karla was directing some volunteers from different agencies. With help from Betty, she had already divided things into piles for the various shelters or organizations. Scotty was helping as well. Clark had been there and had now left to meet with Ian.

Betty sniffed as she helped carry out a box of Sami's clothes. "Karla, I just can't believe she's gone. The rest of the models can't believe it either. I keep thinking she's out on a shoot and will be back in a couple of days. We're all so sad around the agency."

"I know, Betty. It's hard to imagine life without Sami." Karla paused to answer a question from a volunteer. "Is there anything more of hers that you want? You are more than welcome to take anything from these piles and boxes." Karla pointed to the few boxes which were still there. Most of Sami's clothes and shoes had already been picked up. The furniture was being carried out by volunteers from a women's shelter. Karla had some more things that were going home with her.

"Not really, Karla. You already gave me back the small tokens I had given to her, and the photos of her that I liked. I appreciate that." Betty smiled as she walked toward the boxes on the kitchen counter. She touched the soft leather of a golden brown, Hermes bag, which was sitting on top.

Karla noticed her look at the bag. "Betty, would you like one of Sami's purses?"

"Oh, my. No. I mean, yes, I would like one. But, no. They're so expensive. You need to take them."

Karla took nine top-brand, expensive purses out of their cloth wrappings in the box and laid them on the counter. She added four more, less expensive ones alongside. "Betty, look at all these. I couldn't possibly use them all, but I wasn't ready to get rid of them just yet. That would be like getting rid of the last pieces of Sami. Plus, I gave three of these to her. They cost me enough, but each one was for a special time in her life. This one means the most." Karla touched the dark blue, Prada bag. "She had just quit posing for the guy with the porn magazine, and we had arrested him for using under-age girls. This is when she decided she wanted to help other girls who got into this crap.

"I knew she had been looking at this bag, and I dipped into my savings to buy it for her. We celebrated that night at my place. When I gave her the bag, she cried. So, I will most definitely keep this one. Heck, I think I'll start using it now. That way Sami will always be with me." She unwrapped the blue bag and laid it with her black one. She would take it home and put her things in it. "Now, which one do you like? Seriously, I know Sami would love it if you had one of these."

"Oh dear. Are you sure?"

"Absolutely. Pick one you will use, not one you'll just put in your closet."

"I know they're expensive, so I don't want to take one you could sell or give to someone else."

"Betty. You worked with Sami. You were her friend. Now, if money were no object, which one would you pick?"

"The black Chanel one. I've always admired Chanel and thought I might try to buy a wallet or a key chain or something someday."

"Great. It's yours." Karla wrapped it back in its cloth bag and handed it to Betty. "This is for being a friend to Sami and for helping me get through all of this."

"Thank you so much." Betty cradled the purse like it was a fragile piece of china.

The last of Sami's things had been taken away and all that remained were the boxes Karla was taking. Scotty had already carried several to Karla's car. Karla gave one last look around the apartment and turned to her partner. "Well, Scotty. We never did find the ring Sami mentioned. I still think she had it with her. It wasn't bulky like the rest, and she probably thought she could keep it hidden. That's the only reason I can think of that she would mention it was safe." She gestured around the living room. "It's certainly not here."

Betty had been listening. "Did she hide a ring somewhere?"

"Yeah, she did. Or, at least she sent me a note saying she had a ring and would tell me about it later." Karla wasn't going to go into details of the theft, the bracelets, and Gustav with Betty. Betty had only been told that Mr. J wasn't a nice man and probably had something to do with the death of Peter. She didn't know about the connection to Sami. "Why, Betty? Did you ever see Sami wearing a special ring?"

Karla knew Betty and the models had already been questioned about Sami, but sometimes people remembered things at odd times.

"No. I didn't. She usually wore costume jewelry, unless she was modeling for some jewelry store or special brand. I was just curious."

"Thanks again, Betty. I appreciate all your help." Karla and Scotty were carrying the last boxes to the elevator. "Please stay in touch. And, if anything comes to your mind about Sami or the man who called or anything, please give one of us a call. Okay?"

Betty smiled as she walked toward her apartment with her latest treasure. "I will. And, don't be a stranger. We can have a drink and tell tales about Sami."

"Of course." Karla and Scotty entered the elevator as Betty unlocked her door.

# Fifty-Six

GUSTAV HAD RECEIVED the latest text from Mr. Kim, and was enraged. "How the hell does he know about me being at that woman's home? Is he following me? What's with the 72 hours? Now, I have to speed up my plans.

"So much for him not seeing me leave town. Where the hell is he?" Going to the window which faced the street, he cautiously looked out. "Hell, I don't even know who I'm looking for. Mr. Kim. I always assumed he was Chinese. Now, I don't know. And, in this city, there are a lot of Chinese." He moved ever so slightly, looking up and down the street. People of many races and nationalities were on the sidewalks and in cars around his building. "Damn. For all I know, that could be an assumed name and he's actually from South America or Timbuktu."

After the last text, his latest idea of calling Mr. Marsh, telling him he had kidnapped Marta, and was holding her somewhere away from here wasn't going to work. It took too much time to set up and if Mr. Kim was watching him, he'd lead him right to the diamonds. "Nope. I need to rethink this. Is there any way I can speed up the kidnapping plan?"

His mind worked and reworked different scenarios, finally coming to a solution. The only sure way was for her to tell him where they were. They might or might not be in her home. But, he was positive she knew exactly who had them. In order to do this, she was going to have to fear for her life. He'd beat her if he had to, and kill her when he was done with her.

"Now, how do I gain access to her? I'm sure there are police around the neighborhood now. Probably not 24/7 though."

Rubbing his eyes, he took a deep breath. "Think." And, that's when it came to him.

He worked for the next two hours on executing his plan and his disguise.

# Fifty-Seven

**THE TASK FORCE,** minus Marta, was meeting. Ian had several unfinished issues they needed to clear up. He had filled everyone in on the break-in at Clark and Marta's home, including the part about Shadow.

"Lab results came back from Shadow's paw, but they didn't match anything in any of our databases. This probably means we have never grabbed him for anything. If he's that good of a thief, that's disturbing. It also means . . . we still have no idea what he really looks like. That's even more disturbing.

"How about the hotel? Is the envelope with the money still there?"

"Yeah, Ian, it is. No one has even asked about it. What do you want to do?"

"Leave it for another few days or so. I can't help but think he'll be back for it. Or, the woman he's using will be back for it. Keep one guy from SFPD there at all times."

Roger's phone rang, and he excused himself.

Ian had just started to talk about Sami's murder when Roger came back into the room. "Ian, we may have a break. The lab just finished processing the info from the yacht in Sausalito. Our guys had gone over it with a fine toothed comb. They found blood residue on the floor on both the lower deck and on the upper deck.

142

The yacht was clean looking, but no match for our guys and their equipment. They definitely found enough to get DNA.

"They compared it to what was taken from Marta's cat's paw, and they have a match on one of the samples. The other sample matched Karla's sister's DNA.

"This means she was on that yacht before she died. This also means the guy on the yacht, who more than likely killed her, was also the guy in your house, Clark."

Clark nodded.

"But, how and why is his DNA in the blood there? Was there a fight? I honestly don't think Sami was strong enough to hurt him, especially if he was a big guy." Karla shook her head as she looked at Roger.

"Karla, we don't know yet. But, his blood is there along with Sami's.

"Our guys also found a couple of gray fibers. Long ones. They're synthetic, and they might be from a wig. The young man at the marina said the yacht renter was an old guy with long gray hair. He could have been wearing a wig.

"Which means Mr. Johanssen from the restaurant could be the same guy. His hair was long and gray, probably a wig, too. And, even though he seemed old and short, that could all be part of his disguise."

"Okay, Roger. Thanks. Since we now know the same man who broke into your house, Clark, was also on the yacht, we can safely assume he played a role in the death of Sami. We can probably assume he was the one who killed Petrov as well. We know Petrov killed the nephew in Paris. We can probably also assume Petrov and Gustav had a hand in killing Matilda, as well.

"What we don't have, is Gustav. What does he really look like, where is he, how do we find him? He's a master of disguises, so he could be anywhere and we just haven't known it was him. Our informants are good but even they haven't seen him lately. But, it's a good bet he's still here, especially if he is the one who killed Sami, was at the restaurant, and was scratched by the cat when he broke in. He's looking for those diamonds."

"Did you have a chance to enhance Marta's pictures of the yacht, Roger?"

"We did, Clark, and found the yacht to be a match. Marta was right about the towel. It looks like the one that washed up with Sami's body and the one in Marta's picture. The guy on the yacht was definitely dumping something overboard. That towel was part of it. Was it Sami? Who knows? But, more than likely, it was her wrapped in that towel.

"As for a clear shot of the man, not so much. He's looking down in the pictures she took. So, no help there."

"I keep thinking we're missing something. Ian, what else do you have?"

Ian had been reading a bulletin which was handed to him while they were talking. "Listen up. We have news from one of our people there in San Francisco. Mr. Kim has been spotted again with the same older man who sat with him at the restaurant where you and Marta met Mr. Johanssen, Clark. This time, those two were seen meeting with two younger Chinese men at a different restaurant. According to our source, the old man looks more frail than he did a few days ago. I don't know if that is relevant, but something to be aware of.

"Part of their conversation at the first restaurant was over-heard, and I have the transcript of it. Again, I have some transcript of the second meeting. They fit together nicely. Let me read it to you. It's not complete sentences, but the main points are here. There is reference to a man called Gustav. One of the young men apparently followed him to a house where he broke in. He also saw the police arrive. That has to be yours and Marta's house, Clark. One of the younger men gave a sheet of paper to the old man, who looked it over and complimented them. There was some talk of a woman meeting with two men at the first restaurant. That had to be when you met with him, Clark.

"Then, one younger guy gave an address to the old man. At this point, he smiled and acted pleased. At no time were any names mentioned of the participants.

"Our person then missed a bunch of the conversation. Toward the end, money was exchanged. And, this is where things might get better for us. The old man told one of the younger men there would be a bonus if he brought him the bracelet and terminated Gustav. The bonus amount was $100,000.

"Roger, I've already sent the address to you."

"Got it and am sending guys there now. We'll know shortly if Gustav is there."

There was a collective sigh in the room. Clark was first to speak. "Ian, that's the best news we've had in a long time."

"I know you probably all have questions about this, but let's wait to see what Roger's men turn up. Let's take a break. Stay close, everyone."

# Fifty-Eight

**GUSTAV WAS EXCITED.** He was also nervous. His plan was perfect, in his mind. Now, he just needed to carry it out. Looking out the window as he went over things for the last time, he noticed several black vehicles pull up to the curb. "Those are Feds. Who are they here for? It's not possible for someone to tip them off about me. Unless Mr. Kim had a hand in this. But, why?"

Watching two men get out of three different vehicles, he noticed two of the men stayed on the curb. The rest disappeared from his sight. "Damn. This can't be good. I'm glad I took precautions, and they better work. Just in case, I'm going to head into my safe room."

When Gustav rented the condo, he actually rented two different ones on two different floors. He kept the one on the third floor as a decoy and let people see him come and go from there. For that one, he used the renter's name as John Jay, and his credentials matched up. For the one on the fifth floor, the one he primarily used, he rented as Jay Johnson. This one he remodeled slightly to include a safe room with a reinforced door. He also had a small safe delivered, which held his diamonds. He was sure no one ever saw him come and go from this one. He would find out shortly if his ruse worked.

The only regret was that he didn't install cameras anywhere, but that couldn't be helped now. His front door alarm would sound if someone entered, and he would hear it in the safe room.

He waited. This room didn't have any windows, so there was no way he could see the street. He'd just have to wait until he thought the coast was clear. As long as no alarm went off, he knew he was safe. He would use this time to pack up the diamonds he sold to others. Once those buyers had wired him the money, these would be delivered.

His time in San Francisco was about to end. Once he had the bracelets, earrings, and ring from Marta, he'd be on a plane out of here.

After about two hours, he had everything packed up, boxed up, and ready to go. Looking around, he knew he could be ready to leave in less than an hour. His passport that he would be traveling on to Belize, then Cozumel, was handy; the others were packed away. Surveying everything, he decided he would take a chance and see what was going on outside. He had heard no alarm, so he figured no one had entered his condo.

Cautiously, he unlocked the heavy door. All was quiet. Carefully, he walked to the window. Only one black SUV remained at the curb. He could see no one standing by it.

"Hmm. They must be processing my other condo for fingerprints. That will just confuse them. They'll get nothing. Stupid Feds. But, I do wonder who tipped them off and how they found me. I've been so careful."

His phone buzzed with an incoming text from a young lady he hired to pick up the envelope at the Marriott. She told him she picked it up early that morning, she was careful and had not seen anyone watching her, and the envelope was at the appointed spot. His reply to her thanked her and told her where she would find her payment.

"This is good. One more task finished. Only one to go."

What he didn't see was a young Asian man standing in the shadows just down the block. The Feds hadn't seen him either.

# Fifty-Nine

EVERYONE AT THE task force had been working while they waited to hear from Roger. Ian was no longer on Skype, telling them to let him know when Roger came back. He was tuned into the investigation of the condo building from his end, and was working on some other issues.

When Roger entered the meeting room, he wasn't happy. Ian was called to hear what Roger had to say.

"He wasn't there. We're not even sure he lives there. The whole place was too staged. It's like he wanted us or someone to think that's where he lived. Our guys found no fingerprints. None. Zero. They found two pieces of mail addressed to a Mr. John Jay, the name he used to rent this place. In talking with the owner and with the building supervisor, a Mr. John Jay rented this place for six months and paid cash up front. A few people have seen a man come and go from there, but no one could describe him. At least, not any descriptions we can work with.

"One lady said he was cute. Of course, she was about 90. One other lady said he was tall, but one man told us he was old and short. Nothing to go on. Nothing. His credentials matched his rental agreement, but we're still working with the owner to check it out further." Roger shook his head in frustration.

"I can't believe our information was wrong. This informant doesn't mess up. Something's off here." Ian's concern was visible.

As Roger sighed, George, from SFPD re-entered the room.

"People, bad news. Sorry to interrupt, Roger, but I just got word from the Marriott. It seems early this morning, around 3:30, a young woman came in and asked for an envelope they were holding for her uncle. Our officer had just gone off duty and the next one was scheduled to come on in a half hour. So, timing of this was absolutely perfect.

"The desk clerk on duty was tired, and he gave it to her. He didn't remember his supervisor telling him to pay attention to that envelope. The security camera captured her, but it's not the best.

"She's wearing a dark colored mini-skirt, fishnet stockings, and black high heels. She has a large floppy hat which covers almost all of her face, and speaks with a pronounced French accent. The desk clerk admitted he thought she was probably a hooker, according to what he told our guys. She could be about five feet tall, but not much more than that. No idea on age, other than the clerk said she was young-ish. We all know Gustav likes disguises, so she could be any age. I'm not meaning this is him, but he probably had a hand in her attire.

"The desk clerk isn't much help, either. He's a basket case. And, now the envelope is gone. We reviewed street cameras right around the hotel, and we see her exit the hotel and head down the street. She disappears after a block, and we don't see her again."

"Damn."

# $\mathcal{S}$ixty

**THE YOUNG ASIAN** man, who watched the Feds come
and go at the building where he knew Gustav lived, waited until
they were all gone. Then, he waited a while longer. He knew Gustav had rented two separate condos in that building, and he knew
the Feds left without anything or anyone in tow.

But there were things he didn't know. And, that bothered him.
He needed to give answers to Mr. Kim and the old man.

Why were the Feds here? Why were they here at the same
time he was supposed to be here? Did they have the same info Mr.
Kim had? How? Had they been following Gustav, too? He didn't
think so. He never saw anyone who looked like a Fed. So, did they
just get lucky?

He didn't believe in luck.

That meant several things to him. First, somebody tipped
them off. Was it someone he knew? If so, who? Mr. Kim wouldn't
be happy about that. Neither would the old man.

Second, Gustav was in the building. He saw him go in a couple of hours ago, and he hadn't left. He knew about the disguises,
and he watched everyone carefully. He also knew exactly what his
car looked like. Gustav had not left. So, that meant he was in his

second condo. And, the Feds apparently didn't know about that one. Yet.

Lastly, the woman at the restaurant bothered him. Even though she was pretending to be involved in another conversation, he thought she was listening to more than just that. She was with the other men, but something wasn't quite right. She was acting. He'd bet on that. And, that wasn't good.

He didn't want to do anything now. If Gustav had seen any of the Feds or their vehicles, he'd been extra cautious. That was okay with him.

He'd report what went on to Mr. Kim. Then he would wait.

Gustav would come out sooner or later.

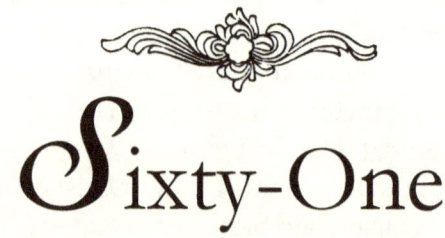

# $\mathcal{S}$ixty-One

WHEN MR. KIM received the message with that information from the young man watching Gustav's building, he turned to the older man. "We have a problem. We may have more than one, but nothing I can't handle."

He filled the older man in on what he learned from their informant. They discussed how and where this happened. "Probably at the restaurant. It has to be her, based on who she was with."

The older man just nodded. "We both knew something was up with those Feds hanging around. Take care of her. Do what you need to." He closed his eyes.

Mr. Kim smiled as he looked carefully at the older man. "I'll make sure we still have the tail on Gustav. I have no doubt he will lead us to the bracelet, and I would bet it is with the woman. Either way, they will both be taken care of."

He noticed the older man looked more frail by the hour, and this bothered him. Taking a deep breath, he knew he had to get the bracelet to have closure for his father.

Mr. Kim bowed to the older man, and left the building.

# $\mathcal{S}$ixty-Two

THE TASK FORCE had ended their meeting for the day, and everybody had work to do. Roger and some of his guys were meeting with the building supervisor about the condo rental. They were double-checking records to see what they could find out about renter John Jay.

Karla and Scotty were headed to Betty's apartment. She called to let them know she thought of something else that might be important.

Ian was working from Paris on other possible diamond buyers, hoping to catch a lead.

Clark was headed home to Marta.

In another part of San Francisco, Mr. Kim was deep in thought after he left his father. He never left anything to chance. He also knew his father was getting anxious, and his health was declining rapidly. More rapidly than he had hoped, as was evident in the last couple of days.

He had researched the woman in question and had found a little about her. She owned a small business and lived in a well-to-do part of San Francisco. He sent the address to his informant, who discovered she lived with a man, probably a boyfriend, who left early the morning he was watching the house. Now all he had to do was schedule an appointment with her. That way she would not be surprised or on her guard when he showed up at her home.

He had no doubt she would tell him where the jewels were, specifically the bracelet. He would also find out who she really worked for. He had his ways. And, those ways always worked.

If the man was living with her, he'd force him to watch, and then he'd take care of both of them. He never left witnesses. He'd have the bracelet and anything else she had. His father deserved that.

Lastly, he'd take care of Gustav. He was tired of him. "Nobody messes with me and lives to tell about it."

# Sixty-Three

**BETTY HAD REMEMBERED** something, but she didn't know if it was important or not. So, she called Karla. When Karla and Scotty arrived, Betty invited them in. Before closing the door, she looked up and down the hallway. Karla noticed.

"What's going on, Betty? Do you think someone is out there?"

"Well, two things are bothering me. I had this dream a couple of nights ago and woke up with this flash. Boom. It hit me. I mean, I just remembered it out of the blue. I have no idea why it didn't register before now. Sometimes, if I'm in a hurry, I just don't pay any attention to authority type figures, especially if they look like they know what they're doing. Do you know what I mean? But, other times, I notice everything. Especially, the second time.

"The first time, this guy. He looked so official and right. Who was I to question him?"

When she finally paused to take a breath, Karla interrupted her monologue. "Betty. Slow down. Who are you talking about?"

"The fireman, of course."

"What fireman?"

"The one who was here earlier. You know, when that guy died in Sami's apartment."

"Okay. Let's start at the beginning. I don't recall a fireman. Please . . ."

Scotty interrupted Karla. "The doorman said something about a fire chief. Remember, Karla? When our guys talked to SFFD, they were told that no fire chief or anyone from the department was here. But, the doorman distinctly remembers talking to the fire department one day and then letting a fire chief into the building for some type of inspection the following day."

Karla was nodding as he spoke. "Yeah, I do remember Ivan talking about some inspector. But what does that have to do with you?" She looked at Betty.

"I was here that day. I had come home just to grab a shawl one of the models needed, hurried in here, and was leaving to go back to work when I saw a fireman standing at Sami's door. While I was locking my door, he turned and looked right at me. Actually, he glared at me. I almost spoke to him, but he had just opened Sami's door and was entering her apartment.

"At the time I thought it was kind of weird that a fireman would go into her apartment. I mean, there was no fire. Not even an alarm or anything. Plus, I thought she was out on a shoot that day. So, why would he go in? I don't think he even rang the doorbell. And, I really didn't hear any fire alarms.

"Now, I was dreaming about fire alarms, and I think that's what woke me up in the middle of the night and why I thought of him.

"Anyway, I was in a hurry that day. Our model needed a vintage shawl to take to a shoot, and I had one. I made such a quick trip home, and completely forgot I was even here. Even if the fireman had turned to me or looked friendly, I knew I didn't have time to talk to anyone. I was really in a rush.

"Do you think Sami was there? In her apartment? Or, do you think he was coming to see the guy who was killed? Why would just one fireman go into an apartment? Why would he go into only one apartment? These are all things I thought of when I woke up. And, no alarm. That bugged me. What if there really was a fire? We have alarms in this building, don't we?" She paused.

"I'm so sorry I didn't remember them until now. Did I mess up?"

Karla and Scotty looked at each other, as Betty continued to talk. The more she remembered, the faster she talked. When she paused again, Karla interrupted. "Betty, slow down. You didn't mess up anything. In fact, it is so great for you to remember this now and call us. Now, we need you to think about that day. Let's start from the beginning. Slow down. Picture the whole scenario in your mind. Start by remembering coming out of your door. Close your eyes.

"Think hard. Can you see the fireman?"

Betty nodded.

"Good. Can you visualize him at Sami's door? Can you see him as he looks at you? How long was he standing there? How long were you standing outside your door watching him? Replay that scene in your mind. Can you see him, Betty?"

Betty nodded.

"Good. What did you see?"

Betty sat still, eyes closed, and started talking. "Well. Let's see. I had just shut my door and looked down the hall at Sami's door. I'm not sure why, but I did. I was surprised to see anyone there, let alone a fireman. Since I was in a hurry, a big hurry, I didn't wave or ask him what he was doing there, or anything. I just made a bee-line for the elevator. He kind of spooked me with his stare." Betty tensed. "But, something made me stop and look back down the hall at him. I didn't really leave the elevator, but I looked out. Do you know what I mean?"

"Yes. Can you describe him to us?"

"He was tall. I remember thinking he was the tallest fireman I had ever seen. He had on a large hat, red jacket and pants, and black shoes. He looked like a regular fireman. Oh, except for his gloves. It was nice that day and it ran through my mind that it was odd he wore gloves inside the building. Plus, they didn't match his clothes."

"Good description. What do you mean, they didn't match?"

"They were white or light colored. Isn't that odd? Shouldn't they be black?"

"Yeah. Do you think they could have been like rubber gloves or were they more like ones you would wear to keep your hands warm?"

"Definitely not normal gloves."

Karla placed a call to the detectives on the case, and was talking with one of them. Scotty had been taking notes while Betty was talking. "This is good, Betty. Real good."

Betty opened her eyes. "But, there's more."

# Sixty-Four

KARLA FINISHED HER call, looked at Betty, and nodded to Scotty to keep taking notes.

"Okay, Betty. What do you mean by more?"

"He was here again."

"What?" Karla and Scotty asked in unison. "When?"

"Today. Well, technically, tonight. I just saw him when I was coming in the building. That's why I called you. It coincided with my dream, and everything just clicked. Sometimes it's like that with me. Two days later something registers. That's what happened here."

Karla made a quick call to get some police presence outside the building. Scotty took a deep breath.

"Okay, Betty. Let's talk about who you saw, what he was doing, and what time this happened. Wait. Are you positive it was the same man?"

Betty nodded. "I was late getting out of work. Some days that happens. Models don't always keep the best schedules, and I have to lock up everything. Yvette, she's the model I was waiting for today, came in about 4:00. I wanted to get out of there by 3:00, but that didn't happen. Anyway, I left right after she put her things away. I was going to go have drinks with a friend, but she had to cancel.

"So, I stopped for a few things for dinner on the way home." She paused.

"What time was this, Betty?"

"I'd say about 4:30 or 5:00. I think I called you at 5:15 when I got here. I was extra careful in the elevator."

"Good. Okay. Tell us what you saw and when you saw the fireman."

"Well, I entered the building. Ivan was busy on the phone, and I just waved to him. I had my purse, a bag from the market, and my shoulder bag. They were heavy, and I didn't want to wait for him to get off the phone. So, I go to the elevator, and I'm standing there waiting. One arrives and there are some people getting off. So, I stand to the side and wait. While I'm standing there, the other elevator arrives and the fireman gets off. Only, this time he doesn't have his uniform on."

"But, you're sure it was the same man?"

"Positive. The first time I saw him at Sami's door, when he looked at me, I noticed his eyes and his forehead. I guess it's working with models all the time, but I notice people's faces. I'm always thinking someone could be a model for something. Sometimes I look at someone and think there isn't any way that person could model anything. So, I notice faces. And, I couldn't forget that stare."

"But you only caught a glimpse of him. And your apartment door is at the opposite end of the hallway. You're sure he was the same guy?"

"Positive. I see so many people every day. I don't miss features."

"Okay. His eyes and his forehead. Betty, what did you see? What did you remember about him?"

"His eyes are the darkest brown, almost black. Very pretty eyes. Not menacing, like you'd think of black eyes. Know what I mean?"

Karla nodded. "Go on."

"And, his eyebrows. Even from a distance, he has distinct eyebrows. Very dark, too. And, heavy. I don't mean uni-brow heavy or gross. I mean like they're drawn or painted on his face. They don't fit his forehead. He has fair skin, really fair skin. These dark eyebrows don't look real. Does that make sense?"

"Yes. Anything else about his face?"

"No. Just his eyes and eyebrows."

"This is really great, Betty. But, was there something else that made you think it was the fireman?"

The doorbell rang, and Scotty got up to answer it. Betty looked at Karla anxiously.

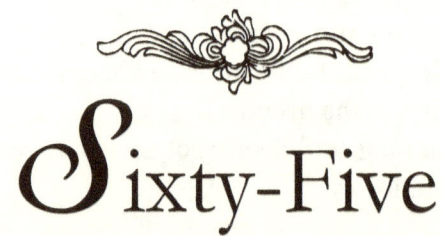

# Sixty-Five

**TWO DETECTIVES WALKED** in and introduced themselves to Betty. She remembered them from the first time they talked to her. Scotty filled them in on the conversation so far.

Betty listened and nodded as Scotty talked. "Think back to tonight when you saw the man again. His eyes, eyebrows, and forehead reminded you of the fireman. Right?"

"Yes. The thing is, I think he recognized me. When I was waiting to enter the elevator, he looked right at me. I could tell he knew he had seen me before. You know how when you see someone you know, you kind of react? Well, that's what he did. He blinked, and his head jerked toward me. That's when I knew it was the fireman."

"Good eyes, Betty. What was he wearing?"

"Oh, this is easy. I know my fashion. I'm in the business, you know. He had on a dark brown, leather jacket. It was real leather. It was kind of worn, but in a good way. Like I said, he's tall, and his jacket fit him well. It didn't look funny or too small on him." She paused, remembering the man. "His shirt was a white oxford with a button down collar. I don't know if it was long sleeved or not, but it almost had to be. Let's see, his blue jeans were a little broken in but not overly worn or tacky; still nice looking.

"But, this is just poor taste. His shoes were not what he should have been wearing with that. They were nasty looking black tennis shoes. Terrible. Just terrible."

The detectives all looked at each other and smiled. Karla spoke first. "This is absolutely fantastic, Betty. Anything else?"

"Well, yes. It's his hands." She looked around the room at everyone's hands.

"What about his hands?"

"Remember I told you about the whitish gloves on the fireman at Sami's door? The reason I noticed his gloves, was the size of his hands. I'm sure his hands were large, or I probably wouldn't have noticed the gloves. When he put his hand on the doorknob, it completely swallowed the knob. Scotty, go put your hand on my doorknob."

Scotty walked to the door and did as Betty requested. His hand covered the knob, but Betty shook her head. "No. His hand did this." She demonstrated by trying to make Scotty's hand larger. "His hand was so much larger. I can't describe it, but it was huge. It ran through my mind that some ad agencies are looking for a man with large hands, and I wondered if his hands were nice and smooth. Sorry. I'm always looking for models."

"No. That's okay. Keep going."

"Well, the man at the elevator had really large hands, too."

"How do you know?"

"He had on a baseball cap. I guess I forgot to mention that. Anyway, when he got off the elevator, right before he looked at me, he pulled the cap down far on his face. He completely covered his eyebrows and forehead, and almost covered his eyes. His hand was huge. Huge."

"That is great. We'll get a security tape from the elevator and talk to Ivan. He might remember seeing him."

Karla got up. "You know what, guys? I still have a key to Sami's apartment. As far as I know, it hasn't been turned over yet to the building. You don't suppose this guy was in her apartment tonight, do you?"

"Yeah, that's exactly what I was thinking. Let's go look." Scotty and the detectives got up.

"One of you stay here with Betty."

Thomas, one of the detectives, nodded his head. "I'll stay.

"I want to go along."

"No, Betty. I want you to stay here. Let's go."

Karla, Scotty, and Frank left Betty's apartment and made their way down the hall to Sami's.

# Sixty-Six

MR. KIM HAD taken a phone call from his informant who had been following Gustav. After learning of his latest venture, he told him to continue following Gustav.

Turning to the older man in the room, he had a puzzled look on his face. "This is interesting, Father. Gustav made a trip to the apartment where Petrov was killed. We know it belonged to the model who drowned. We don't know how all three were connected."

"He is positive it was Gustav?"

"Yes. He was disguised, but still easily recognized. He has been under surveillance all day."

"So, Gustav did kill both of them?"

"I would say, yes he did. But, he took a risk going back to that apartment. He must still believe something is there. Which means . . . he really does not have my diamonds or your bracelet."

"Did he find anything there?"

"We're not sure. The police and others have been in that apartment off and on for days. I would have to say nothing is still there. And, he seemed upset when he left, according to our guy."

"Where is Gustav now?"

"After he left the apartment, he made a stop at a UPS store and came out with an envelope he tucked into his jacket. Then, he went back to his condo and is still there. He'll continue to be watched."

"Fine. When are you taking care of the woman?"

"Tomorrow. I know her schedule. She has a meeting in the morning, and I have set up an appointment at her house at noon. She will be there. I'll finish her then."

"Good. We need to be gone shortly. My time is running out."

"Understood."

# Sixty-Seven

**GUSTAV WAS CAREFUL** when he went to Sami's apartment. He was positive no one followed him, and he made sure the doorman was busy and other tenants were getting on the elevator before he entered. This allowed him to access the elevator without having to put in a code or use the call button.

On the fifth floor, no one got off. After making sure no one saw him, once again he easily picked the lock. As he expected, the apartment was clean, but he checked every little space. His hope was that there was some secret hiding spot everyone else had missed.

No such luck. Once again, he was furious. "Where are the rest of the diamonds? Where the hell is my ring?" Carefully, he wiped down anything he had touched, pulled his cap down low on his head, entered the elevator, and prepared to leave the building.

When he exited the elevator on the ground floor, he recognized the woman who lived on the same floor, just down the hall, from Sami. Before she could get a good look at him, he hurried to the street.

After a quick stop, he returned to his condo and replayed the trip in his mind.

"Damn. She looked right at me. Is there any way she could have recognized me? I can't believe she got enough of a glimpse of me that day. Yet, her eyes showed some glimmer that she had seen me before. But, how? My back was to her the first time I was there." Back at his condo, Gustav was pacing and talking to himself. His frustration was mounting with each step. "I'm going to have to tie up that loose end. Can't have her remembering me. Can't take that chance."

Walking past the envelope he picked up at the UPS store, he opened it. Satisfied the money was all there, he repackaged it and put a label on it. "Time to deposit this. Then, I have to take care of business and get the hell out of town."

He sat down to think.

# Sixty-Eight

KARLA, SCOTTY, AND Frank returned to Betty's after
another search of Sam's now empty apartment. Frank dusted for
fingerprints on door knobs, but they were wiped clean. "Someone
was here. There is no way I wouldn't get some print off of one of
these. Movers, police, somebody would have touched something."
He moved into the kitchen and did the same with the refrigerator,
stove, and microwave. "Nothing here, either."

"I don't suppose we could get any worthwhile prints off the
elevators. I have no idea how many people have touched those
buttons."

"Yeah. I doubt it. That was a couple of hours ago. Let's go back
to Betty's. I think we're done here."

After locking up Sami's apartment, the three headed down
the hall. Thomas and Betty were sitting at the dining room table,
Thomas was sketching, and Betty was nodding her head. "A little
darker." They looked up when the three entered.

Karla noticed the drawing. "I was going to suggest a sketch
artist downtown, but this is fantastic. I didn't know you could do
that, Thomas."

"It's a hobby of mine. I paint and draw to relax and have just
started sketching people." He turned the drawing of a face toward

the rest of them. "Betty has a great memory and a wonderful eye for detail. It was pretty easy working from her description."

The detailed face of a man stared back at them on one page. On a second page, drawings of hands.

"My goodness, that's amazing. Great work, both of you. We need to get this out right away." Frank picked up the drawings.

"Yeah. We need to get a copy to the boss and to Ian. Everyone needs to see this. I don't suppose you have a copy machine here, Betty?"

"Of course, I do. I use it all the time when I have to copy contracts the models left somewhere. Come into my office."

Once copies were made and emailed to the task force, Karla made some extras for Frank and Thomas to take with them. "Okay. I think we're probably done here. Betty, we need you to be extra careful. Don't go anywhere alone. I'm going to give one copy to Ivan to be on the lookout for this guy. I can't believe he'd come back a third time, especially since he probably didn't find anything this time. But, you can't be too careful."

"Do you think he realized you had seen him?"

"I really think so, but you don't think he'd come here to my place, do you?"

Karla sighed. "Who knows? He may be desperate enough. Frank called Sandra, a female officer, who will stay here for a few days. She should be here soon. We don't want you to be alone. Okay?"

Betty's buzzer sounded, and she gave Sandra the code to enter the elevator. In a few minutes her doorbell rang and Karla introduced her to Betty. Once everything was explained, the rest of them got ready to leave.

"You are such great help, Betty. We'll be in touch. Thanks for all your good observations."

As they left, they all discussed the luck of Betty's sharp eye for detail. "This may be our break, guys."

"I know. I just hope nothing happens to her."

"Yeah. We need to keep her safe. This guy is determined. And, brave enough to come back. Why does he think Sami had his diamonds?"

# $\mathcal{S}$ixty-Nine

**THE FOLLOWING MORNING,** Ian called everyone in for a quick meeting, focusing on the drawing from Betty. "This is great news, people. With everything Betty told you last night and this sketch, this is our first big lead. This drawing has been distributed to every law enforcement agency in the world. We know he's good at disguises, but this has got to help. Clark, you had the best view of who we assume was Gustav that night at the restaurant. Is this him?"

"If you add bushy gray hair, bushy eyebrows, and tons of make-up, it's a plausible match. His eyes were really dark green, but that could have been contacts. It would be really hard to disguise dark, dark brown eyes into another color. And, both Marta and I thought his eyebrows were fake.

"His hands did seem large. But, like we said, he kept them either under the table or kind of in a fist. George, you had a good look at him, too. What do you think?"

"I agree with your observations. It could be him. But, I'm not positive. Sorry."

"No worries, guys. It is disturbing that he would come back to Sami's apartment, though."

"Does he think Petrov or Sami hid something there that the police wouldn't find? I mean he has to know we've been all over that place. Right?"

"Karla. You're right. Why did he come back there? What are we missing? It's obvious he doesn't have the bracelets and earrings, because Sami sent them to you. We still don't know what she was talking about when she mentioned the ring, though. It must have been one of the ones listed that are significant. There are at least three that are valued in the upper six figures. My guess is, she saw or had one of them. We're assuming Petrov stole the bracelets, earrings, and at least one ring, maybe more, from Gustav. Question is . . . where is the ring she mentioned? She said it was safe. I know you think she had it with her.

"But, is it possible Petrov kept it? Maybe he hid it in the apartment, didn't tell Gustav about it before he was killed, and then Gustav went back to look for it.

"My gut tells me this guy is approaching his limit. He's desperate. Desperate enough to do something hasty. We have to assume Mr. Kim is his main buyer. If Gustav doesn't have what Mr. Kim wants, he might be putting the screws to Gustav. Do we know if he's still in town and if he's still in the market for diamonds? Especially the ones Gustav stole?"

"Yeah. He's still here. With the Ghost."

"Any news on that guy?"

"Our tail got a good look at both of them and sent some photos, but they were blurry. We're working on the description, comparing it to what our sketch artist is working on. We'll have that shortly."

# Seventy

MR. KIM HAD his appointment set. He called and told her he wanted to meet with her in person, and that he was leaving town right after he met with her. She was reluctant, but agreed to the appointed time.

He knew there was a man staying with her, but he didn't know if he was there today or not.

He didn't want to leave anything to chance or for her to recognize him, so he was heavily disguised. He owned several passports, and picked a look from one of those. Today, he was conservatively dressed in a navy suit. His smooth, short, dark hair had been covered by a light brown, curly wig, which had been tailor-made for him. Light powder was applied to his face to lighten it up a shade. Dark-framed glasses completed his look.

In his pocket were his gloves and his tools. The handgun was not registered to him or to anyone; the knife was sharp; his Taser was handy, and the roll of tape had no fingerprints on it. His rented, non-descript car was parked down the block. He had not seen another car parked near her home.

Precisely at noon, he rang her doorbell. When she opened the door, he nodded, thanked her for seeing him on such short notice, and reintroduced himself as Juan Cortez, a magazine editor who needed to visit with her about an upcoming trip to France.

He spoke with a Spanish accent. She welcomed him inside, offered him coffee, and led him into her office.

"You have a lovely home. Do you work from here?"

"Thanks. Yes, I do. I'm freelance, so it works well. How long have you been in San Francisco?"

"I've only been here for a week on business. Now, I need to get home."

"I see. Okay, what can I tell you about France that you might not already know?" She still didn't really understand why he was here.

"Does anyone else live here with you?"

Thinking to herself that he was getting kind of personal, she nodded to him. "Sometimes. Why?"

"I just wondered if anyone was here." He looked around as he said it.

"Not right now." Red flags were going off in her head, and she moved toward her desk as she talked. Her cell phone was laying on her desk. She could hit one button to summon the police if his questions continued along this line. "I blocked out 15 minutes for this meeting. What did you need to know about a trip to France?" She was all business.

He saw her move to the desk, and noticed her phone. He didn't want her to reach it or to sit down behind her desk. Moving quickly, he blocked her from reaching the desk. She started to turn toward him as he grabbed her arm. Holding it tightly, he pushed her away from the desk. She struggled. He twisted her arm.

"What are you doing? Please let go of my arm."

His grip became firmer, as his fingers dug into her arm, and he twisted harder. "I don't think so. We are going to talk."

Her training kicked in and she swung at him with her leg. He saw it before it happened and moved away from the kick. Then, she tried to punch him with her other arm, and he deflected that, too. Several more moves by her were easily stopped by him. His grip remained on her arm. She was smaller than him by at least a foot, and no match for his deceptive strength and his martial arts training.

"What do you want?" Her breathing was heavy as she tried to fight him.

Jerking her toward him, he grabbed both arms and held them behind her. She spat at his face and kept trying to get free. Securing both of her arms with one hand, he reached into his pocket for his handgun. She took this opportunity to try and twist away from him. Almost succeeding in freeing herself, she ducked when she saw his fist. She wasn't quick enough as he connected with her cheek. He pulled her closer, took the handgun, and placed it against her temple. "I said, we're going to talk. Got it? Nod if you understand me."

Her cheek throbbed, but she nodded, still planning on escaping him. The desk wasn't that far away. Slowly, he moved her toward a love seat, never letting go of the tight grip on her hands. Once again, she kicked out toward him and connected briefly with his thigh.

"Damn you." He had had enough. His handgun dealt a blow to the side of her head, and she slumped away from him, dazed but not unconscious. He picked her up, placed her on the love seat, pulled a cord out of his pocket, and tied her hands behind her before she could regain her senses.

Her eyes tried to focus on him as her brain tried to focus on the situation. Giving her no time to react, he grabbed the Taser, and gave her a jolt. As the shock shot through her, she fell limp against the back of the love seat, shaking. He took this opportunity to finish tying her up.

Coming to after several minutes, she struggled with the rope binding her hands and feet. Then, she lashed out at him verbally. "What the hell is going on? Who the hell are you? Let me go."

Calmly, he sat down opposite her. "You have something of mine."

# Seventy-One

AT THE TASK force meeting, a sketch artist brought her computer and was working with both the sketch from Betty and the one made from the blurry photo from the restaurant. She was adding features, subtracting features, making each one appear older or younger, and showing what each would look like with various disguises. Those were being compared to the security camera from the apartment building where Betty and Sami lived.

Everyone was gathered around her, looking and trying to catch something that would help narrow down the looks of both Gustav and the Ghost, as they were calling him.

Roger was on the phone with the company that owned the condo building where they thought Gustav lived.

Ian was on the phone with another informant and just joined the conversation via Skype. "Listen up, everybody. I've just been informed there has been a young Asian man watching the building where we thought Gustav lived. My source tells me this man has followed the man we assume to be Gustav, from the building and then back. He was disguised, but close enough to our description of Gustav.

"The Asian man hangs around outside the building, almost unnoticeable. Gustav has to live in that building, even though we didn't find anything including fingerprints in his condo. Roger, do you have anything?"

Roger had just hung up. "I got part of your conversation, Ian. Just got off the phone with the manager. This is curious and may explain some of what is going on. Two different men, two different names, rented two different condos in the same week in this building. Both paid cash for six months. One is the condo we were in, rented to a John Jay. The one where everything looked too perfect, too staged, and no prints on anything. The other one was rented to a Jay Johnson a few days later. So, no red flags. But, it was stupid simple on his part. Once I told the manager why we needed more info, he double checked info and just now called me. The bank on record is the same bank for both renters. That's not unusual, until you look at the account numbers. They're identical. The manager and owner didn't realize this, as the account is legit. Once he started looking deeper, he noticed it.

"We need to investigate that other condo, but I don't want to spook him. We need to plan this one better. I've already cleared everything with the manager. He'll have a key for us at the front desk. I'm working on a warrant, but that may take until tomorrow. And, now that you've been told someone else is watching him . . . why? Who will we be alerting when we go in? Do you think Mr. Kim is involved in this somehow?"

Clark had been half listening as he was looking at the sketches. "Sorry to interrupt, but I need to call Marta. She might have a better feel for the looks of this one sketch." He placed a call, and left a message when she didn't answer.

Roger continued. "I think we need to look like possible renters. That way we won't spook the watcher."

"Probably a good idea, Roger. But, we need more than just two people going in. If the young Asian man is, by some chance, working for Mr. Kim, he'll spot us right away. We don't need that, and we don't need Mr. Kim knowing what we're doing. Ideal situation is that we'd like to catch up with him and the Ghost he's been seen with.

"I think it would be best if we go in as city or building maintenance people. George, can you get us a truck or two and some uniforms? We should be ready to go tomorrow as soon as we get the warrant."

George made a phone call. "Got it. You'll have everything whenever you need it. They're waiting for you downtown. They'll have eight uniforms with them."

"Great. Thanks. In addition, two of you can go in as potential renters. Roger, can you set up that?"

"On it."

"Okay. This is how it's going to go down."

# Seventy-Two

FOR OVER AN hour, Mr. Kim had been questioning her and then torturing her when he didn't like her answers. He was becoming more frustrated by the minute with her answers, or lack of answers. She was in bad shape from the beatings. Holding a gun to her head hadn't worked, either. This was going nowhere. He had nothing.

He had swept her phone off the desk, shattering the screen. At one point, when she was unconscious, he looked around her office for a wall safe, and found nothing. She refused to answer if she had one, and that had caused him to leave an ugly bruise on her face. He was going to have to up the torture. He was running out of time.

"Last chance to answer my questions. Where are they? Who do you work for? Where is Gustav?" He waved his gun in her face.

"I told you. I'm a photographer. I have no idea what you're talking about." Defiantly, she looked at him through swollen eyes. Her face was bloody, he had broken her arm when he grabbed her, and she had been in and out of consciousness. But, she was determined to ignore the pain in hopes he would leave her alone. She was afraid that wasn't an option.

Looking at his watch, he stood up. "When does your boyfriend get home?"

"I don't have a boyfriend." Her answer put him over the edge. This was becoming ridiculous and he was tired of her.

"You have left me no choice." Calmly, he picked up his handgun, held it to her head one last time, and fired a shot. As blood spattered everywhere, she slumped onto the love seat. Just as calmly, he meticulously worked his way through her home. He found nothing he was looking for.

"Damn. I hoped she had the bracelet and the diamonds." He again looked for a wall safe, and finding none, went about wiping everything clear of his prints. He hadn't touched much, but he wiped the areas where his prints could have been. "Well, at least she won't be in the way any longer. Now, time to finish with Gustav. We've already stayed here too long."

Earlier, her phone had buzzed with a message, but he wouldn't let her answer it. "According to my source, she does have a boyfriend. I need to leave before he gets here."

Carefully, he opened the front door, wiped the knob clean, and made his way to his car.

Once back at the hotel, he gave the news to his father.

"Do you think she told you the truth?"

"Yes, I do. If she knew, she would have said something. Or, her eyes would have given her away. But, it's over. She's history. Now, to Gustav. And our jewelry."

His phone rang. Listening to the caller, he turned to his father when he hung up. "He is still watching Gustav's building. No activity. He will stay on him.

"I want to take care of him tomorrow. He will be followed and subdued. Then, I will dismiss the informant and work on him myself." Mr. Kim and his father were careful not to use names of their informants. Once their work was finished for Mr. Kim, he would dispose of them anyway. They didn't know this.

"I have called for our plane and it will be ready as soon as we need it. Do you have everything else you need?"

"I do, my son."

# Seventy-Three

CLARK HAD PLACED a second call to Marta, which also went right to voice mail. "What's up? I don't like the feeling I'm getting. I'm going to head home and see if everything is okay. See everyone tomorrow. What time are we meeting?"

"That's fine, Clark. We're all done here for the day anyway. Tell Marta hello.

"Everyone, let's meet back here at 7:00 a.m. Roger, will we have the warrant by then?"

"Yep. I've contacted the building manager so he knows when we'll be there. He'll put notices in mailboxes today telling everyone the water department will be working on a building leak all day tomorrow, and residents should try to avoid being in the building. And, George has everything ready from the city's water department for us.

"We'll also have city cops on the street. That's common practice, so no one who is watching will think anything about that. They'll be directing traffic around the trucks. There will also be three detectives in street clothes, just in case we need back-up. Everyone will be armed, although not noticeable. We will start watching the building at 6:00 a.m. If Gustav leaves, we'll be able to follow him. If not, we'll grab him in his condo."

"Is there any reason we shouldn't be watching him now?"

"We can, if you want us to, Ian."

"Just a minute. I'm getting an urgent message. Let me get right back to you. Nobody leave yet, please."

Clark was anxious to see what was going on with Marta. It wasn't like her to not answer her phone. Especially after the break-in and when she knew things were crazy with Gustav and the diamonds. He decided he needed to go and knew Ian would understand. "Roger, I'm heading out. Marta's not answering and that bothers me. Call me if anything changes. Otherwise, I'll see you all at seven tomorrow morning."

Roger nodded. "Yeah. Go ahead. I don't blame you for being nervous. See you tomorrow."

# $\mathcal{S}$eventy-Four

CLARK LEFT AS everyone else talked about the plan for the following day. After just a couple of minutes, Ian came back on Skype. His face registered shock and anguish.

Roger picked up on it immediately. "What's wrong, Ian?"

Ian took a deep breath. "Is Clark there?" He could hardly get the words out.

"No. He was having trouble getting ahold of Marta, so he left a few minutes ago. He was worried about her. Why?"

"I need you to call him and have him come back. It's imperative he be here. I have to be the one to tell him about her." Ian rubbed his face. Everyone in the room immediately stopped what they were discussing and focused on Ian. Silence reigned. Concern was on the faces of everybody in the room. Nobody wanted to look at one another, afraid of what they'd find out.

"Who and what?"

"She died." Ian looked at his hands, obvious he wasn't going answer a frustrated group without Clark there. "Get Clark."

Puzzled and afraid, Roger looked at the rest of the group, took a deep breath, and placed a call to Clark. Luckily, he had only made it to the parking garage, and hadn't left yet. "Ian just got some bad news and wants you here. Can you come back for a few seconds?"

"Sure. Any idea what's going on?"

"I'm not sure." Not wanting to alarm Clark, but he also wanted to warn him this was serious. "He said he wants to tell us all, but especially you. He said somebody died. He wouldn't say who until you got here."

A chill went up Clark's spine, his heart plummeted, then raced. He tried to place another call to Marta as his fingers fumbled with his phone. That call, like the others before it, went to voice mail. He didn't even leave a message. He couldn't.

"I'm on my way." Thoughts spiraled through his brain. None of them good. *Why wasn't Marta answering her phone? Did someone really die? Who? Where was Marta? What the hell was going on? It can't be her. It can't.*

He rushed through security, barreled into the conference room, and glanced at the screen. The minute he saw Ian raise his face from his hands, he felt a bigger chill go through his entire body. Ian's look of utter despair was heart-wrenching.

Walking toward the table took an eternity. Looking at the faces in the room confirmed his worst nightmare. His chest was heaving. *It's Marta. Something happened. Why did I involve her in this anyway?*

Everything felt in slow motion as he finally looked toward the screen. Digging deep and finding his voice, Clark managed to speak. "Ian, what the hell is going on?"

Ian stared at all of them. Finally, he shook his head slowly. It was an effort for him to talk. The room was like a tomb. Everyone was holding their collective breath, trying not to look at Clark.

Ian had composed himself and apologized to the group. "Clark, I am so sorry. This just hit me hard. Harder than losing anyone has ever hit me and . . ."

"Ian. Damn it. Who died? Is it Marta?" Clark pounded his fist on the table as he stood directly in front of the screen. No one made a sound. He couldn't breathe.

"No, it's not Marta."

Clark sank into the chair closest to him, and released his pent-up breath. Everyone took a deep breath, glad it wasn't Marta but still wondering who Ian was talking about.

Silence stretched as Clark's mind turned from relief to frustration with Ian. "Get to the point, Ian." No one had ever heard Clark raise his voice, let alone at Ian.

Ian looked directly at the screen. "I apologize. Again. Today we lost a dear friend of both Clark and me. The rest of you have met her at one time or another. She was one of our finest and most diligent agents. Many of you knew she had been working a case that was indirectly related to this one. She has been following Mr. Kim for over two years, and was the one who was giving us intel on The Ghost. Her name was Mary Wong."

Roger gasped. Clark shook his head. "Not Mary. What happened?"

"You may not have seen her at the Italian restaurant the other night, but she was there. Later, she was at a Chinese restaurant, following Mr. Kim and The Ghost. She was Chinese and spoke fluent Mandarin, which is why we've been able to find out as much as we can about Mr. Kim.

"Clark introduced Mary to me about ten years ago, after they worked together on a case. Mary jumped at the chance to work for me, and I trained her myself. She was like a daughter to me, when she wasn't in the field. Her brother is big in the tech world there in Silicon Valley and has a fantastic home on Nob Hill. He has been working undercover for us as well, mostly in cyber security. She stayed with him when she was in the area.

"Today, she was tortured and shot in the home she shared with her brother. Another agent went to her house to pick her up for a meeting, and found her. It was a deliberate murder, based on the scene he found."

# Seventy-Five

RELIEF FILLED THE room, yet sadness showed on the faces. Everyone knew the danger, yet something like this was hard to hear. Ian continued.

"We're still piecing together how and why. Was it Kim? Based on the type of torture, we're assuming it was. If so, why did she let him into the house? She knew what he looked like. So, was he disguised or did he force his way in? What we do know is, he was there for approximately two hours; he tortured her, and then he shot her. Our second agent had just turned the corner when he saw a car leaving from about a block away. For some reason, he decided to follow the car. He has no idea why. All the windows were dark, so he could not see anyone in the car.

"He followed for several blocks, until the car pulled into an underground parking ramp at the Ritz.

"But, he got the license plate and ran it. It's a rental, rented to a John Sun, all IDs fake. We're working with the Ritz as we speak.

"Anyway, our agent goes back to the house and finds Mary. That's when he first called me. We have agents and SFPD there right now.

"Again, I apologize for dragging this out, but I was hit hard, harder than I've ever been when losing an agent. Clark and Roger, I need to talk to you some more. The rest of you, keep working your angles and help out at the crime scene if you can. We'll recon-vene tomorrow. In the meantime, do we have the building secured where we think Gustav lives?"

"Yeah, we do. I've got everything in place for tomorrow, once we get the warrant. I've also got some guys watching it tonight. Nobody is coming or going without us knowing about it."

"Thanks, George.

"And, thanks to all of you for understanding."

Karla received a call from Ivan and left to see what that was about.

# Seventy-Six

GUSTAV DIDN'T KNOW what made him extra cautious. But, something did. He had had this feeling one other time, and he had narrowly escaped with his life. That was a dangerous situation he didn't want to repeat. He would always remember that day in Mexico.

He was in Mexico City, and had just relieved some tourists at the Ritz of their jewelry. It was stupid of them to leave everything in plain sight. Especially after they flaunted it at the swim up bar. I mean, who wears diamonds that large to a pool? Posing as room service, he was in and out of their room in just a few seconds. With the jewelry.

Something had caused him to pause in the hallway. He didn't know what, but, it was a strong feeling. He had ducked into a side corridor, just as two gunmen broke down the door of the room he had just been in. He wasn't sure what happened next, as he high-tailed it to the stairwell and sprinted down all 17 floors in record time. Winded, he tried to slow down as he exited the hotel and hailed a cab. He was sure everyone could hear his heart beat.

Once back at his hotel, he had packed up everything, and left the country. Later, he read about some drug dealers who had their diamonds and emeralds stolen from the Ritz. They were still looking for a waiter who delivered room service. "Good thing I was heavily disguised."

Now, sitting in his condo, he had the very same feeling. Cautiously, he looked out the window, and noticed a thin, young Asian man across the street. He sat on a bench, smoking, and reading a newspaper. "He's been there before. He's too young to be Mr. Kim, but he probably works for him. That son-of-a-bitch really is watching me. Okay. Time for action. I'll get to the old broad first and take care of her, and then tomorrow the other one. They WILL talk. I have no doubts about that. Mr. Kim isn't ever going to get the bracelet or earrings. The deal is off! Nobody, and I mean nobody, follows me."

He went to work on his disguise. Then, he double-checked his packages of diamonds, other jewels, and the gold and platinum. Confident everything was ready to go, he labeled the packages. These would be sent to his address in Puerto Rico. A courier service was coming tomorrow to pick them up from the concierge desk in the building. He would take them there tomorrow morning before he got the bracelets, earrings, and ring from the woman. Process of elimination told him she either had them or knew where they were.

When he first moved in, he had found a service elevator to the parking garage underneath the building. It was used mostly by workmen and delivery people, not the residents of the building. They all used the more modern, better looking one. This one was older, but still functioned, especially for him right now. Once he had everything the way he wanted, he exited his condo, took the stairs to the top floor, and found the door to the service elevator. Once in the parking garage, he got in one of his cars, pulled a cap down over his forehead, and exited the garage, going the opposite way from the man watching the building. "Perfect. He didn't even see me."

After a quick stop, he made his way to the building where Betty lived. He had checked the doorman's schedule and knew he was due to leave shortly.

# Seventy-Seven

**ACROSS THE STREET** from Gustav's condo building, the young man received a call from Mr. Kim. After listening to his questions, he responded. "No. I have not seen him all day. Of course, I have been watching the front door. Yes. There is a garage, but no one has exited it in the last hour."

Mr. Kim was furious. "Something is going on. He spotted you and did not want you to see him leave."

"No. There is no way he spotted me. I have been very careful."

"Not careful enough. Okay. Come to the meeting place. We will regroup." Mr. Kim abruptly hung up.

The young man didn't like the sound of Mr. Kim's voice and had no intention of meeting him. He knew what Mr. Kim did to those who messed up their assignments. He wasn't going to be one of those casualties. He disappeared down the street, caught the bus, booked a flight on his smart phone, and headed to the airport. He was on an airplane in two hours.

Mr. Kim relayed the conversation to his father.

"This is not good. What is going on?"

"I have some ideas and will have to follow up on them myself. Our worthless informant is long gone by now, I am sure. I will have to watch Gustav myself. He will be confronted in his condo, where the mess will be contained. It will all happen tomorrow."

"Good."

# Seventy-Eight

GUSTAV STOPPED AT a florist, bought the largest bouquet they had, filled out a card, and headed to the building where Betty lived. He was dressed as a florist delivery man in blue jeans, light blue shirt with the name of a florist, dark tennis shoes, and a name tag that read Joe. His windbreaker jacket had tape and rope in the pockets, and his handgun with a silencer was in the back of his jeans. No one could see any of that. His car was parked in a ramp about a block away.

Walking into the lobby, he greeted Ivan. "Hey man, hope I got the address right. These are getting heavy. And, I'm starting to sneeze."

Ivan looked him over. "Who is the delivery for?"

"A Betty Martin. Says this address with the number 502 on it. Ring any bells?" Gustav looked at the card as he read it to Ivan.

"Yeah. Betty lives in 502. But, I'll take them and call her."

"Nope. My instructions were to deliver them to her myself. Not supposed to hand them off."

"Our policy is for deliveries to be left with me. Who are they from?"

"See, that's the deal. The San Francisco Police Department is sending these to her. Talked to them myself and they were real firm on me delivering them right to her door. I won't get paid unless I do exactly like they said. They told me to tell you that and you'd understand. Guess she had some trouble or something. Maybe it was a friend of hers who had trouble. Can't remember exactly.

"So, can I go up and surprise her?"

Ivan knew it was against protocol, but if the police were sending flowers to Betty it was probably because of something to do with Sami's murder. They were good friends, and Betty worked where Sami was a model. He debated in his mind, and then decided it was okay. He'd have the guy sign in, so he had his name.

"Hey, man. These are getting heavy. Can I go?"

"Yes. You may. First, sign in right here." Ivan handed him a log, and Gustav signed an unreadable scribble.

"Thanks. I appreciate it. I need the commission on this delivery. Hey, what time do you get off? Want to have a drink?"

"No thank you. I am meeting a friend for dinner at 7:00 and don't want to be late. Tell Betty hello." He looked at his watch. "I have to leave in a couple of minutes. Just sign out when you come back down. Okay?"

"Sure. Thanks again. I owe you." Gustav headed for the elevators.

# Seventy-Nine

**GUSTAV LOOKED AT** the floor during the elevator ride to the fifth floor. Walking up to Betty's door, he listened. Hearing nothing to cause him alarm, he pulled his weapon out from behind his back, and rang the doorbell.

Nothing. He rang it again and knocked loudly. The only other apartment on this floor belonged to the model and he knew no one was there. Still nothing. Once more, he rang the bell and knocked even louder, almost pounding on the door.

"Strange. The doorman didn't say she was gone."

Setting the vase of flowers on the hallway floor, he took out his tools, put on some gloves, and picked the lock. Carefully, he opened the door. The dark foyer opened to a dark living room. Only a small nightlight in the kitchen gave off any muted light.

"Hmm. Maybe she's not home yet. But, it's 7:00. Maybe she's out to dinner. I'll sit and wait for a little while. I can look around here, just in case. Then, I'll start the ball rolling to get my stuff from Marta. It's freaking brilliant of me to get Mr. Marsh out of the way first. I'll send him off on a wild goose chase and then I can take care of her." He mumbled as he walked around.

After two hours of searching her entire apartment, looking for any signs of something Sami would have given her, he found nothing. And, still no Betty. "Damn. Where is she?" He looked around her apartment for signs which would explain her absence. Nothing was written on her desk calendar, no notes were lying around. "I really can't wait any longer. I'm going to leave the flowers, but take the card. I can always call her at work to ask about them. Maybe she would agree to meet me for coffee and I can take care of her then." He left and headed back to his condo building, dropping his car in a parking ramp a few blocks away.

About the same time he was wondering where Betty was Ivan was sitting at dinner with his friend. All of a sudden, he looked up and shook his head. When his friend asked what was wrong, Ivan told him about the flower delivery. "I completely forgot. Betty told me this morning she was going out of town for a few days. Remember, I told you about the model who lived in my building? And, the guy who was shot? Well, the model's sister is a cop and wanted Betty to go stay with her daughter for a few days, until things calmed down. Betty told me she would be gone until next week.

"She thought the police were getting close to finding out who killed both Miss Sami and the guy who was staying with her. She also figured that's why they wanted her to be somewhere safe.

"That flower delivery man won't find anybody home. I wonder what he'll do then. But, . . ." Ivan didn't finish his sentence as another thought came to him. "Oh, my. I think I messed up. I need to call Miss Karla, and tell her." Ivan pulled out his cell phone and placed the call to Karla.

Telling Karla the whole story about this evening, he hung up, and looked at his friend. "Karla and the detectives will take care of it. They know the code to get into the building. She thinks the flower delivery man was not real. She knows the SFPD would not send flowers to someone through any old florist. I never even thought about that. Stupid me."

His friend patted his hand. "I'm sure it will work out. Don't get too worked up about it."

"No. We're finished with dinner. I need to go to the building and make sure everything is okay. I'll see you next week. Okay?" They parted ways and Ivan headed back to the building, arriving about the same time as two police cars and Karla.

# $\mathcal{E}$ighty

**KARLA LEFT, GREATLY** relieved it wasn't Marta who was killed, and headed to Sami's apartment building. Two detectives had been talking to Ivan, who was glad to see her.

"Ivan, good thing you called me."

"Miss Karla, I am so sorry I let that delivery guy go up to Betty's apartment. He showed me the card, and it said San Francisco Police Department on it. I didn't even think. That was so stupid of me. I even knew Miss Betty isn't there. She told me you wanted her to visit her daughter. I don't know what I was thinking. It was late and . . ." Ivan was clearly distraught, and Karla tried to comfort him.

"Ivan, no need to worry. You did the right thing when you called me. Why don't you stay right here and let us do our job? We'll be back down in a few minutes. Okay?" She motioned for the detectives to follow her upstairs.

Ivan sat down at his desk and waited. He knew Betty would be okay. But, he was hoping the delivery man screwed up. He started searching through the security tapes, looking for the ones from tonight. Seeing the delivery man come into the building, he noticed his hat was covering most of his face, and that he looked away from the front camera. Then, he pulled up the elevator one. This one wasn't any better at capturing his face.

He did notice his hands, though. "I'll have to show this to Karla." The last one he looked at was when the man exited the building. "I have to show this to her, too. He was here a long time. What was he doing?"

Karla, Scotty, and the other detectives had entered Betty's apartment and were looking around. One detective started dusting for fingerprints. The vase of flowers sat on the table. "Well, he was here. But, Ivan said there was a card from SFPD on it, and there's nothing like that here.

"And, this is odd. No prints of any kind on the vase. We'll have to ask Ivan if he wore gloves. If not, he's wiped the vase clean." He was working his way around the apartment, going from room to room. The others waited. "Well, there are plenty of prints. Probably belong to Betty, though. It is odd the doorknob was wiped clean. So, he was looking for something."

"But, what? I mean what did he think she had?" Karla had a puzzled look. "He only talked to her at the agency. Or, at least, that we know of. And, how the hell did he get in here?"

Scotty spoke up. "Probably picked the lock. Maybe he didn't think she had anything. Maybe he was going to get rid of her. If he thought she spotted him or remembered him, he might have been tying up loose ends. What better way to gain access to a lady's apartment than to bring her flowers? And, I'll bet he knew exactly what time Ivan was leaving. He probably gave him some song and dance to get access to the elevator."

"Aha. That's why the card he had on the flowers said SFPD. Ivan would have thought nothing of that. It would probably seem legit to him."

The detective, who had been dusting for prints, had gone into the hallway, dusted the outer doorknob, and had gone down the hallway to the elevator. Coming back to the group in the apartment, he had a smile on his face. "We may have gotten lucky. Her doorknobs are clean, but the button in the elevator for this floor has a big ol' print. It very well could be him."

Karla grinned. "Betty left yesterday after work and I wouldn't think there would have been anyone else on this floor. It's just her and Sami's apartments on this floor."

"I'll get these to the lab and catch up with you guys later."

They all headed back down to Ivan.

"Miss Karla, look at these." He pulled up the tapes and played them for the detectives, pointing to the things he thought were odd.

"Good work, Ivan. By the way, do you know of anyone who would have been on Betty's floor in the last day or so?"

"No. Why?"

"We may have found a fingerprint. Did you go up to her floor at all?"

"No. Let me look at my log." Ivan pulled out the sign-in book and looked. "There has been no one here at all, except for residents." He turned the book to them to see.

"Okay. Thanks again for letting us know so quickly. We may have caught a break. Now, you can get back to your evening, Ivan." Karla, Scotty, and the detectives left as Ivan closed up everything.

# Eighty-One

**GUSTAV ALWAYS HAD** several plans, in case he needed them. That's how he survived in this world of his for this long. When he dropped off one of his rental cars, it was in a ramp a few blocks away. He never used the same pattern more than once, if he could help it.

By now, he was no longer dressed as the floral delivery man. Now, he was disguised as a janitor. Through a side door, he had slipped into the underground parking area for his building. For several minutes he waited in the far corner. Two other cars came in and parked, and one left. The drivers never noticed him.

He noticed something which bothered him, however. At least one police cruiser, possibly two different ones had driven slowly past the building. They were just visible from where he was standing. "This is odd." He waited a little longer.

Then, not wanting to attract attention, he carefully made his way to the service elevator, and up to his floor. Seeing nothing to cause alarm, he entered his condo, keeping the lights off.

Looking at the street, he was sure the man sitting on the curb and the one talking on the phone at the end of the block were cops. "Why? Why are they here now? Did Mr. Kim send them? Is he working with the cops?" He laughed at the absurdity of his thought. Then, he turned serious again.

"Did the police somehow follow me? Is that woman, Marta, connected to the cops? I find that hard to believe. And, yet, they're here. Well, I've left no evidence. I need to move the time frame up and get out of town. To hell with Mr. Kim."

Making sure he had his things packed up for shipping, he spent the next hour wiping down the apartment. He had a method and stuck to it. The boxes which were being shipped would be left at the front desk. The night manager would take them, put them in a locked room, and take them to the courier in the morning. He wasn't worried about the night manager recognizing him or questioning him. He was just a college kid trying to earn a few extra bucks, and Gustav would give him a nice tip. Gustav would be disguised anyway.

The other, smaller boxes and his luggage would go with him to the rental car in a second ramp. That was supposed to happen tomorrow, but the presence of the cops changed his plan. He'd have to go tonight and figure out where he was staying. He thought about calling a cab, but didn't want to risk causing any suspicion. He'd have to rearrange some things, but he could do that.

He'd put the rest of the plan in place first thing in the morning. Then, he was gone for good.

Taking some time with the disguise he was wearing tonight, he smiled to himself. His disguise for tomorrow was packed in his luggage.

Looking around the condo one last time, he mentally checked off his list. He had cleaned it, wiped it down, packed up everything, and was ready to go. He had already made one trip to the night manager, who was half-asleep, but gladly took his tip. Back upstairs, he completed his new disguise, and headed for the underground ramp.

"Perfect."

# Eighty-Two

MR. KIM AND his father were cleaning up things on their end at the same time.

"Tomorrow morning I'll go to his condo, take care of him, and retrieve the bracelet and my diamonds. Then, I'll meet you at the plane. Our pilot will already be there. It shouldn't take more than three hours, once I leave here. I've called for the driver to pick you up and take you right to the airport. Will that be okay?" His father nodded. Mr. Kim hoped he could make it.

"I've brought in another informant, who is watching the building, just in case something strange happens. I'll also take care of him before we leave. That way, there are no traces of anything left here."

His father placed his hands in front of him and once again nodded. "I will be fine, and will see you at the plane. This entire masquerade has gone on too long. Justice needs to be served, and before I die I deserve what is mine. It will finally happen. Now, I must get some rest." He stood up, held onto the back of the chair, and slowly started toward the bedroom.

Mr. Kim started to say something just as his phone buzzed. Puzzled, he looked at the number. "This is the informant. He was not supposed to call me at this number unless something drastic happened."

He answered, listened, and asked a few questions. When he hung up, he looked at his father. "This is puzzling. There are plain-clothes police around Gustav's building, the street is being blocked off, and city utility trucks are arriving. Our informant walked into the building, posing as a renter, and asked the man at the desk what was going on. He was told they are preparing for a water leak to be fixed in the morning, possibly lasting all day." Looking puzzled, he paused.

"That would explain the trucks and the street closure, but not the cops. There is more to this than he was told." Mr. Kim looked at his father, who had sat back down.

"What is he going to do, now that he's been seen and could be identified?"

"I told him to change his look and then to remain close to the building. I want to know more about this." As he was talking, his phone rang again. After this conversation was finished, he hung up and turned to his father again.

"Gustav has left the building by way of a side door out of the underground parking. It was our good fortune our informant went that way to change his clothes. He would not have seen him from his vantage point on the street. This is troubling.

"Even more so, Gustav had two pieces of luggage, a backpack, and a satchel. He's moving out." Mr. Kim paced while his father waited for him to continue.

"He's on the move, because our informant followed him to a parking ramp about a block away, where he got in a car different than the one he had been using. He drove to a hotel close to Fisherman's Wharf, where he checked in. Our informant followed in a cab."

"What did you tell him to do?"

"I told him to stay out of sight, across the street, and watch. When he leaves, I want to know. We now know the car, and he will be easy to follow."

"Where is he going? Why did he leave his condo?"

"I can only assume he discovered the cops and realized something was up. My gut tells me he still doesn't have the bracelet and is going after the woman who does; the one who's house he broke into. I will follow him, once he leaves the hotel. I am positive he would not leave town without it."

"Once I am finished with him, I will handle the informant. Then, we leave."

# Eighty-Three

IAN HAD FINISHED telling Clark and Roger everything he knew about Mary Wong and her murder. They were stunned by the brutality of it. Her brother was an agent as well, and was called in off of a surveillance case. Understandably, he was devastated. Ian and Clark knew her best, but Roger had met her as well.

Marta finally called Clark back, telling him she had been with her accountant and had her phone on silent. "What's up?"

Clark sighed. "You have no idea how afraid I was. I honestly thought Ian was talking about you. I was certain I would never see you again."

"What happened?"

Even though she didn't know her, he filled her in on Mary's murder. He didn't go over all the grisly details with her, but told her this was a calculated, brutal murder.

"Where are you now?" Hearing she was almost back home, he told her to wait for police before entering the house. "Are the police anywhere around?"

She told him she had just pulled into the driveway and one police cruiser was parked out front. Once the officer had cleared the house and found nothing out of place, Marta called Clark back. "It's all clear, and no one has been here."

Relieved, Clark refocused on Ian's reports.

"Okay, a few more details. Mary had given Interpol a detailed list of Mr. Kim's contacts, his dealings, and his schedule. In the last year, she put 'clients' in touch with him to purchase diamonds. He had never seen her, to her or our knowledge. However, something tipped him off to who she was. Possibly, having her in both restaurants this week did it. She was positive she could pull it off." Ian sighed. "Apparently not. Something caused him to notice her.

"Anyway, she first noticed the older man a few months ago. The Ghost. She thinks he might be related to Mr. Kim., based on a transaction she observed in Paris. This was about two months ago. The two of them were at a restaurant where Mary was posing as a bartender. She overheard a conversation which led her to believe something big was going down.

"It could have been this heist.

"The Ghost was visibly upset when Mr. Kim mentioned a man's name. Mary didn't get the name. Shortly after that, the Ghost asked the maître d to call a cab, and Mary got the address from him. We've had that house under surveillance since then. Mr. Kim hadn't been there, but last week the Ghost had a driver pick him up and take him to the private terminal at de Gaulle. We're assuming that's when he arrived here, and we don't know if they came together. We don't know where Mr. Kim was at that time."

"Sorry to interrupt, Ian, but do we know any more about the Ghost?"

"Up until an hour ago, we didn't, Clark. We obtained a warrant and have been going over the home and grounds where he lived. Mary handed us a goldmine when she got that address. I'll know more shortly."

# Eighty-Four

**THROUGHOUT THE NIGHT,** several agents and police were keeping an eye on the condo building where Gustav lived. Nothing seemed out of place, and no one resembling Gustav left the building. Everything was in place for the supposed water main leak and repairs for the next day.

In his hotel room Gustav was wrapping up the last details of his stay in San Francisco. Everything was in place for his encounter with Marta, including his disguises. Once he was finished with her, and he had his diamonds, he would head to the airport. His boxes had been left with the manager at his condo and they would be picked up and sent to his address in Puerto Rico. He would check his two large suitcases, and carry on his laptop bag and another small bag. "Things are good. Those diamonds will be where they should be. Mr. Kim can go to hell. I will have my insurance policy and my ring." He talked as he wiped down every surface. "I will wear gloves from here on, so I leave no prints in this room."

In the Pacific Heights area, Clark hugged Marta and reiterated his concern. "I love you and I thought I had lost you. I honestly don't know what I would have done."

Marta smiled. "I probably should have answered my phone or at least looked at it. And, I am so sorry to hear about someone else being killed. These diamonds are really becoming deadly, aren't they?"

"Yeah. I know all of us want this to end before someone else gets killed." He kissed her again.

"Do you think he's still at the condo? Do you think he'd try anything again so soon?" Marta had brought wine and dinner out to one of the terraces.

"I honestly don't know. Part of me says he's too confident to think anything could happen to him. Yet, another part says he's already long gone. Maybe that's wishful thinking on my part."

"What about Mr. Kim? Is he still here? Has Ian told you anything more about The Ghost's place in Paris?"

"We all think Mr. Kim is still here. After all, he doesn't have the diamonds. Or, at least we're pretty sure he doesn't. We have the ones Gustav left at the hotel for me, and the big ones Sami sent to Karla. We're still missing a lot of smaller ones. I say smaller like they're tiny. They're not. And, we have no idea on the ring Sami mentioned. It has to be the largest of the ones Matilda had. But, again, it's all speculation. Gustav could have it, Petrov could have had it. We just don't know. Karla really thinks Sami had it in her purse or somewhere on her and it's at the bottom of the Pacific. At this point, I tend to agree.

"Ian doesn't have good information on Mr. Kim right now, but if he really wanted the diamonds, he's still here. He may even be watching Gustav, if he's still around. I guess we'll all know more tomorrow."

Marta took another sip of wine. "How's Karla doing? I haven't talked to her for a few days."

"She's doing okay right now. But, that's because she's busy with this task force and trying to put closure to Sami's death. When we're all finished, she'll have a hard time adjusting to her being gone."

Clark finished his dinner just as his phone rang. When he finished his call, he turned to Marta.

"That was Roger. He's been working with the Ritz. Remember the rental car registered to John Sun? That's the name of the man driving away from the home where Mary was killed. Anyway, John

Sun was also registered at the Ritz. But, get this. The description of the man renting the hotel room fits The Ghost. The manager described him as an old, really old, Asian man who was frail and hunched over. Not what you'd expect a killer to look like."

"Was he alone?"

"He was when he checked in, according to the manager. But, one time he saw a younger Asian man outside the door to the old guy's room. When the younger man saw the manager, he turned away, got in the elevator, and left. The manager just thought he was strange at the time. Now that the FBI has been questioning the manager, he brought up that incident."

"What was the younger guy doing?"

"The manager had been called to a disturbance in a room just down the hall from the old guy's room. These rooms are on the concierge level, very expensive, and very exclusive. So, when someone calls about an issue, the managers respond. He described the younger man to Roger, and it fits with the description Mary had of Mr. Kim. The description of the old guy also fits with her description of The Ghost, only he appears to be getting frailer. Perhaps he has health issues."

"If the room is on the concierge level, wouldn't the younger man need a code to get to that floor?"

"Right. That's another thing the manager brought up. It was disturbing to him that just anyone could get to that floor. But, Roger is positive they're connected and that they are Mr. Kim and The Ghost. He suspects the younger man is Mr. Kim and that he is staying there with The Ghost."

"So, what happens next?"

"Roger's men are watching the room and the hotel. They'll question anyone who looks like either of these men. If nothing happens tonight, they will knock on the door in the morning and ask if they've heard any disturbance. That way they can get a better look at whoever is in that room."

Marta had picked up the dishes while Clark was talking to Roger. They were finishing their wine as they talked. "Do you think you'll ever find all of the diamonds?"

"I sure hope so, but a lot of things have to happen just right. What do you say we forget about diamonds for tonight and concentrate on each other?"

"I'd like that."

Clark pulled Marta to her feet, kissed her, and led her into the bedroom.

# Eighty-Five

"FATHER. I WILL call you in the morning. Our driver will pick you up and take you to the airport." He gathered up his things and walked toward the door.

"Be careful, my son. Get my bracelet."

"I will. By tomorrow this will all be finished. Good night." He hated to leave his father alone. He looked so frail. But, it couldn't be helped. Soon this would be finished. He was betting the bracelet would help improve his father's health.

Mr. Kim made his way to the parking garage, unseen. He did, however, notice two plain clothes police in the lobby. "Timing is good."

After retrieving his car from the valet, he drove to the hotel where his informant had reported Gustav was staying. It would be an uncomfortable night in his car, but worth it to get his father's bracelet and to put an end to Gustav.

His plan was to follow him in the morning. If he headed toward the airport, he would intercept him, and take the diamonds. If he went somewhere else, that meant he didn't have the diamonds and was going after them. If that was the case, he would wait until he had them and then take action.

He settled in.

# Eighty-Six

IAN HAD A briefing early the next morning with the task force. Everyone had their assignments and knew the plan for the condo building. If they encountered Gustav, they were to take him alive, if at all possible. His two condos would be searched at the same time, and there were police in the parking garage, as well as on the roof.

If he was in neither of the places, the forensic team was standing by to process each condo. Security cameras would be accessed. Neighbors would be questioned. The night and day managers would also be questioned.

Other officers would be in various locations on the street, keeping an eye out for anything which looked out of place.

"Okay, team. Let's roll. Roger's got the lead."

Everyone left to do their job.

Just as Clark drove up to the parking garage, his phone rang. It was the one he used as Mr. Marsh. He hit the talk button, but didn't get a chance to say a thing.

A gruff voice started speaking immediately. "Mr. Marsh. Your girlfriend has my bracelet, and I want it back. Therefore, I have your girlfriend."

For the second time in two days, Clark's heart plummeted.

The voice continued. "If you want to see her alive you will do as I say. Do we understand each other?"

"Yes. What do you want?"

"Do not and I repeat do not contact her. She will die if you do. Her phone rings, she's dead. Her phone gets a text, she's dead. Got it?"

"I want to talk to her."

"No deal. You talk to her, she dies. Are we clear?"

"Yes." Clark swallowed, his mind was working overtime. His chest tightening, he had trouble breathing.

"Okay. You are to go to Jack London Square in Oakland. There is a coffee shop next to the Potomac's dock. Got it?"

"Yes."

"Tell no one where you are going, or you'll never see her again. Make sure no one follows you. I am watching you. Remember, do not contact her. If her phone rings, I will put a bullet in her head.

"I repeat. Are we clear?"

"Yes." Clark could hardly speak.

"I will give you further instructions once you are there. You have one hour to get there."

"How will . . ." Clark didn't have a chance to say anything more as the caller had hung up. At first, he felt helpless. He took his other phone out of his pocket, and looking around the parking garage, he made a call to Ian. He had to hope there was no one watching him.

"Someone's got Marta. I assume it's Gustav." He relayed the rest of the conversation to Ian, all the time searching for anyone who might be watching him.

"Hold on. Let me call Roger."

He came back to Clark in a couple of minutes. "Karla is on her way to Oakland, too. She'll be there before you. Do as he says, and be careful. We will not contact Marta, and I suggest you don't either. He could mean what he says. Okay?"

"Yeah. Got it."

"Be careful and get going. Roger knows what's going on."

# Eighty-Seven

ONCE GUSTAV MADE the call to Clark, he finished adjusting his disguise, packed the remaining items, and left his hotel room. He drove to the Pacific Heights address, the one he had already broken into once. This time, she would gladly open the door for him. He was sure of that.

As he pulled out of the parking ramp from the hotel, he didn't notice a car following him at a discrete distance.

Mr. Kim, the driver of that car, was sure he knew where Gustav was headed.

Gustav drove past Marta's home and then parked about a block away. He noticed a police car leaving the area. His luxury rental car did not look out of place in this neighborhood. Looking in the mirror one last time, he put on his hat as he exited the car and started to walk toward Marta's house.

Mr. Kim parked down the block the opposite way. When he saw Gustav, or who he assumed was Gustav, get out of the car, he was puzzled. Very puzzled. "What the hell? Is this him or does he have someone on his payroll?" He continued to watch from a distance.

Gustav looked around. Seeing no other police cars, he made his way to the front door, and rang the doorbell.

When Marta answered, he nodded his head. "Officer, did you forget something?" She looked past the man into the street, wondering why he was back so soon.

"I'm afraid I have some bad news. May I come in?"

"Of course." Marta opened the door wider and turned to allow the policeman standing on her doorstep to enter. That was the opportunity he needed. With the weapon he had been holding behind his back, he struck her in the back of her head, and she started to fall. He grabbed her and pulled her inside. Then, he shut the door, and dragged her into her office just off the foyer. She was unconscious.

Pulling out his tape and plastic ties, he first bound her hands and feet. Placing tape over her mouth, he then dragged her to a chair, and tied her to it. Her head sagged toward her chest. She didn't move. Satisfied she wasn't going to get loose, he put on gloves and started searching the house. He was looking for a wall safe.

Starting on the first floor, he moved all the paintings he could and found nothing behind any of them. A few were secured to the wall and he left those alone. He looked for locked cabinets that could hold a safe. Nothing. Once the first floor was searched, he started on the second floor. He kept an eye on the time. He needed to keep Mr. Marsh away from the house.

He stopped and sent two text messages that should do the trick.

Marta was still out, slumped in the chair. Unseen, Shadow watched from behind her desk.

On the street, Mr. Kim was still puzzling over why a cop would be the one driving Gustav's car and why a cop would come to this house.

# Eighty-Eight

**KARLA WAS AT** the coffee shop and noticed Clark come in. He did not acknowledge her, but sat down to wait. When the appointed hour was up, he began to get nervous.

His phone buzzed with an incoming text. "Buy a ticket for the Potomac. I will meet you on board."

He responded but, didn't receive an answer. The USS Potomac, docked in Oakland, cruised the bay once or twice a day. This historic ship, once belonging to President Franklin Roosevelt, was a landmark here in this area. Cruises filled up fast,

Clark wasn't eager to be onboard and away from land, unavailable to get anywhere quickly, but the next text gave him no choice. It was a blurry photo of Marta, all tied up. She was sitting in a chair, but he couldn't tell where. All he could see behind her was a wall. He hoped she was still alive.

He scribbled a note on a napkin for Karla and left to buy a ticket. He had no idea if he was being watched. Karla picked up the napkin, read it, and threw it away with her coffee cup.

Just before they closed the ticket office, she also bought a ticket and boarded.

# Eighty-Nine

**DOWNTOWN, THE TASK** force had made their way into the first of Gustav's condos.

"Just like before. There is nothing here to indicate anyone lives here. No prints, no personal items, nothing." Roger had called Ian. "Any news from Clark?"

"No. But, I didn't expect any. He's being cautious. We don't know what this guy might do, and we can't afford to take any chances. Especially after Mary."

"Right. Everyone here knows not to call Marta for any reason, but I didn't tell them why."

"Okay. What's the status there?"

"I have guys ready to go into his second condo. We're also talking to the manager. He can't seem to get ahold of the kid who works the night shift, though. I guess he's a college kid and probably in class. I'll keep you posted."

Roger had just entered the second condo. One team was dusting for prints, and another team was taking photos of all rooms. "Wow, Roger. Look at these rooms. These are some interesting renovations. Between the mirrors, closed up window, serious locks, and alarm, this room is literally a safe room. No cameras, but look at the quality of all this stuff."

Roger looked around. "Any prints, so far?"

"None. But, we're just getting started."

Roger had been looking as he walked around. "I'm betting this alarm is connected to the door. Right? He could be locked in here, no one could get in this room, and he would have an alarm to let him know if anyone entered the condo. But, how would he know the intruder was gone? Like you said, there's no camera." He walked around some more.

"Who knows? Maybe he just outwaited any intruder."

"Or, maybe he never had an intruder. This was just in case someone entered. Keep at it, guys. Let me know if you find any prints. At this point, I'm not hopeful."

# Ninety

AT MARTA'S HOME, Gustav was still searching diligently for a safe or somewhere she could have hidden the bracelet and the rest of the diamonds. He emptied drawers, looked in the pantry, and went through kitchen cabinets. He searched closets, drawers, and dressers in all bedrooms. Bathroom cabinets were emptied. Marta was still unconscious, tied to a chair in her office. Shadow was out of sight, still watching from behind the desk.

On the street, Mr. Kim was keeping an eye on the house and on any traffic going by. "I don't get it. That car is the one my informant said Gustav drove. Could he have been mistaken? Or, did he give me bad information on purpose?

"And, why is a cop staying inside her house so long? He must be hanging around so nothing happens to the woman. But, why? Is something going down? Do the cops have intel about Gustav that I don't have? Why would a cop drive that car? It's not a cop car. Not even close."

He made a call to his father. "Any news from our informant, or has he skipped town?"

"Nothing. Why?"

Not wanting to upset his father, he told him he was just asking. "Are you ready to go to the airport? The driver should be there shortly. Okay?"

"Yes. I have wiped down every surface I may have touched since you left. The sheets and towels are packed in a box. I am just about ready to go. I will see you in a little while."

His father sounded weaker to Mr. Kim's ears. "Good. Now, sit down and take it easy while you wait for the driver. We have a long flight."

Mr. Kim continued to watch the house. "I'll give this another few minutes or so and then find an excuse to go in." He settled in and kept his eyes on the front door.

# Ninety-One

ROGER TOOK A call from his men at the Ritz, telling him nothing had happened on the floor they were watching. No one had come or gone from the room they were keeping an eye on, either. He told them to keep watching, but not to go in just yet. The issue with Marta had changed the way they were going about grabbing anyone.

He talked to the team processing the condo belonging to Gustav. They had plenty of information, dozens of questions, and as of yet, no fingerprints. "This is just bizarre. He had to go to a lot of trouble to wipe everything down." Roger was on the phone with Ian, telling him about the safe room, the safe, the alarms, and things they uncovered.

Just then, Charles, one of Roger's team interrupted him. "The manager and the college kid who manned the desk at night need to talk to you. Sorry to interrupt."

Roger nodded to him. "Ian, I've got to go. I'll call you back."

"Okay. Where are they?"

"In the manager's office, downstairs." He led the way.

Roger walked in and noticed that the college kid looked like he could get sick at any minute. He looked at his boss and then at Roger. "Did I do something wrong? I mean, the picture they showed me looks a lot like one of the renters. But, I swear I didn't know he was wanted by you guys. I mean, he was really nice to me. Even gave me a big tip. I'm going to college, so any extra money is great. But, I really didn't do anything wrong. I just took his packages and meant to call the courier like he asked me to. I just forgot and I was late to class. Am I in trouble with him? Am I in trouble with you?" He rubbed his palms on his pants, took a deep breath, and looked at his boss.

Before he could get his second wind and continue, Roger offered him a chair. Putting his hand on his shoulder, he spoke to him. "Easy. You're not in trouble with anybody." The kid visibly relaxed for a second, then a look of fear came over his face.

"The packages. I forgot to get them to the courier. Is he going to be mad? I really need this job."

Roger once again placed his hand on his shoulder. "Let's talk about the packages. Then we can talk about the man who gave them to you. Okay?"

The kid nodded.

"First, when did the man give them to you?"

"Yesterday. Well, late yesterday. I was sitting here when he brought them to me."

"Okay. Do you know what time?"

"He made three trips. It was about 3:00 or 4:00, I think."

Roger looked at Charles and nodded. "Good. What did he ask you to do with them?"

"Call the courier and have them shipped. But, I forgot. I was late to class this morning." The kid hung his head and rubbed his hands over his cheeks and face. "I'm so sorry." He looked at his manager.

"Don't worry. Where did you drop them? We can try to intercept them."

He shook his head. "That's just it. I didn't. I forgot. They're still in the trunk of my car."

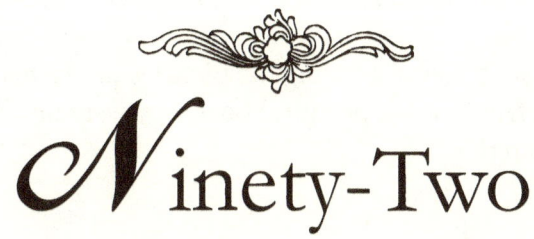

# Ninety-Two

**ON BOARD THE** USS Potomac, Karla walked up to Clark and in a voice meant to be overheard, greeted him. "Hello. I'm with public relations. Is this your first time on the Potomac?"

Clark immediately knew she was trying to see if anyone was overly interested in their conversation. "Yes. It's quite nice. What can you tell me about it?"

She took his arm as she maneuvered him toward some seats as they talked, away from everyone. "I've looked at all the passengers, no one looks suspicious or out of place. And, certainly no one looks like him." Her voice was low and hushed, but she kept smiling and nodding to Clark, motioning with her arm.

"That's good." His voice was still a little louder as he looked where she pointed. No one had shown any interest in them. He lowered his head and spoke softly. "What now?" He looked at his phone. "I have a bad feeling. He was supposed to meet me on board. I looked at everyone, too. Unless he has a gofer, we're in a bind."

"What do you want to do? I don't want to jeopardize Marta, but we have to do something or get someone to her."

"I will text him and see what he says." Clark sent a text to the number. They waited. After 10 minutes, he sent another text. "This is bull. I think he set me up. But, why? Where does he have her?"

Karla called Ian to fill him in. He told her about the development at the condo and to wait for a little longer. He was still concerned about Marta, remembering what had just happened to Mary.

Clark paced, never noticing the picturesque scenery, spectacular waterfront, or the beautiful boat they were on. "Damn it. What's he doing?"

# Ninety-Three

**ROGER COULDN'T BELIEVE** what the kid just said. "You have them in your car? Where is it?"

"Downstairs in the garage. I can get them."

Roger, Charles, the manager, and the kid made their way to the kid's car. Roger had left a quick message for Ian, letting him know what they were doing. When the kid opened his trunk, four large boxes sat there. "I thought he only gave you three."

"Yeah, he did. But, this morning another one was sitting on my desk. I don't know how it got there. Here, let me take them out."

Not knowing what was in them, especially after all the precautions and alarms in Gustav's condo, Roger was taking no chances. "Stop. Don't touch them." He put his arm on the kid's.

The kid jumped back like he had been slapped. His eyes bugged out as he looked at Roger.

"We don't want to disturb anything that might not be good. And, we need to see if there are any prints, other than yours on them." In reality, he had no idea if they were rigged to blow up or just what they would find. He made a call to the bomb squad, who had been waiting nearby in case one of the condos was rigged. Charles called some SFPD officers to guard this part of the parking garage.

Once the bomb squad arrived, they instructed the others to wait behind the armored vehicle while the packages were inspected.

"What are they doing?" The kid was curious about the robot, and yet a little frightened by the two men in rubber suits and helmets. He tried to see what was going on.

"The robot is looking for wires that might trip something. One of the men is using a machine to get a look at anything obvious inside. It's not an x-ray, but close to it." Roger nodded as one of the men motioned to him.

"We don't have any trip wires and nothing seems to indicate explosives, so we're going to pick these up and open them in the vehicle. You can stay here if you want. We'll know shortly what's in them." He carried each box into the armored van, closed the door, and watched as the robot slit the tape and lifted the flaps of each box. Nothing happened, so one of the men entered the van. After he was finished removing everything from the box, he came to Roger. "We're all clear here. Nothing to worry about. But, you'll be pretty amazed at what's in these boxes. Where do you want them?"

He had put everything back in the boxes and was in the process of carrying them out of the van. Roger looked at the contents of the first box. "Whoa. I can see what you mean. I believe this is what we've been looking for."

Eyes bulging and mouths hanging open, the manager and the kid looked at each other and then at Roger. "Is that real? I had this stuff in my trunk all day. I don't get it." The kid had a dazed look.

"Yeah. They're all real." Roger made a quick call to have the boxes moved to the task force office. As two SFPD detectives loaded them up, Roger motioned to the manager and the kid. "Let's go to your office. We need to talk."

Back in the manager's office, Roger turned to the two men. "We've been working on a high profile jewelry heist. This is only part of the operation. I need to have your cooperation on this.

For now, you can't say anything to anyone about this. Okay?" He looked at the two men, who nodded. "I'm serious. There are still some people in danger and any leaks could harm them greatly, even kill them. If that happens, you will be liable. Understood?"

Once again, they looked at each other and nodded. "Okay. I need a statement signed. I'm trusting you."

The manager spoke up. "Are we in danger, too?" The kid looked like he swallowed a lemon, whole.

"We don't believe you're in danger. But, we're not positive and there are others who may be impacted by all of this. For now, we're going to have an officer accompany both of you for a few days. Once we're convinced we have everything wrapped up, the officers will leave. Do you have any questions?"

Two SFPD officers had entered the office and were introducing themselves to the kid and to the manager. The two were still in shock at what they had seen in the parking garage. "Can I go to class?"

"Yes. Go about your normal routine until you are told differently. You'll just have one of these guys following you."

Both men nodded.

# Ninety-Four

"**NOW I WANT** to show you some photos. Look carefully and let me know if anything jumps out at you." Roger placed photos of Gustav on the desk. The kid looked at all of them, not recognizing most of them. He went back to one and studied it. "I saw a person who looked a lot like this one day. I was going off duty kind of late and had just gotten into my car in the garage. A car drove in. The lady driving was odd looking. I remember she looked like she had on a wig, but had it on crooked. Does that make sense?

"Anyway, I dropped my phone on the floor. By the time I picked it up, I watched the person get out of that car. She wasn't a lady anymore. She was a man."

Roger had been listening. "What do you mean?"

"It was the same car. But, her wig was gone. So were her glasses. In her place was a man with a gray ponytail and a Giants cap. As he stepped out, he put on a dark blue jacket."

"Good eye. Anything else?"

"Well, I didn't see him after that." He looked at another photo.

"This one could be the man who gave me the boxes to mail. Except, he's heavier here." He pointed to the midsection of a man in one photo. "But, his eyebrows are the same. And, his hands are the same. He had really large hands. I remember thinking I had never seen hands quite that big before."

"Great job. Okay. I'm going to leave you to get acquainted with your new best friends. Let me know if you have any questions. I'll be back before you leave." Roger made a phone call to Ian as he headed back up to Gustav's condo.

# Ninety-Five

GUSTAV HAD SEARCHED Marta's house, more than once. Frustrated, he walked into her office.

Marta had started to come to, but still couldn't figure out exactly what had happened. She knew she was tied up. She couldn't move. But, why? Where was she? Then, one-by-one, pieces started coming to her. Some made sense; others just confused her.

For some reason, she sensed rather than saw someone walk into the office, but she kept her eyes mostly closed. Even though she didn't know why, she didn't want whoever it was to know she was awake. She kept her head lowered and tried to relax.

Her arms had lost most of their feeling and her wrists hurt where the plastic ties were cutting in to her flesh. Her legs and feet were tingling as they slowly lost feeling. A pounding headache had started at the back of her head where she was hit, and had now made its way to the front. Every time she swallowed or tried to blink, shooting pains reverberated throughout her entire skull. She had trouble breathing, and the tape over her mouth almost caused her to panic.

Out of the corner of her eye she saw Shadow. She hoped he wouldn't get hurt. Tears started to roll down her cheeks.

Gustav walked over to Marta and stood in front of her. "Wake up." He shook her arm, and then lifted her limp head. When he ripped the tape off her mouth, she gasped and took a gulp of air.

She had no choice except to look at him. "What do you want?" Her voice sounded scratchy and mumbled to her ears. "Who are you?" She sniffed and swallowed as more pain invaded her head. Trying to moisten her swollen lips, she realized she had no saliva.

"I want what is mine. The bracelet. The diamonds. The ring."

It took a few seconds for Marta's brain to register what he said, but she didn't understand it. What was he talking about?

"What? I don't know what . . . I don't have it." She was slightly aware she wasn't making any sense. But, so far, nothing had.

Glaring at her with wild eyes and a heaving chest, he made a fist with one hand and smacked it into his other hand. "Of course you do. Now, where are they?"

Looking at his wild eyes and heaving chest, she jumped when his hands smacked together. Somewhere in the back of her mind, his hands created an image. But, she couldn't quite put that image with anything that made sense to her. She shook her head as she looked down.

Putting his hand on her forehead, he forced her to look up at him. She was beginning to panic, and tried to calm her heart rate and breathing. It didn't work. Somewhere inside her, she wondered why a policeman was doing this to her. She couldn't quite put the pieces together. Why did a policeman want diamonds? Or, wasn't that what he asked? Had she misunderstood him? She was so confused, and her whole body hurt.

"Look at me. You wore the bracelet that night. What did you do with it?" He grabbed her jaw and squeezed. "I'm done playing games. I need all the jewelry she gave to you."

Marta's fuzzy brain was still trying to piece together what he was talking about. She blinked. Who? What night? What jewelry did he think she had? Her jaw hurt where his hand was. She tried to shake her head. "I don't know what you're talking about." Her words came out mumbled.

In an instant, he let go of her jaw and slapped her face.

Her head snapped back, her eyes widened, and she glared at him. With more clarity, his large hands triggered a memory. More intense pain took over that memory and radiated through her head and face. "Stop it. I really don't know what you mean. Please, just tell me what you want."

"As if you didn't know. I know she gave the bracelets, earrings, and ring to you. I saw the bracelet on your arm. Now, where are they? I'm running out of patience. And, I'm running out of time. That means you're running out of time, too.

"For the last time, where are they?" He moved a few steps away.

Marta was still trying to figure out exactly what he was saying as images of bracelets and jewelry wove their way into her brain and then just as quickly, they floated out. Jumbled thoughts about Paris, a large bracelet on her arm, a restaurant, a man with large hands, and Clark hovered, not yet making sense. She shook her head as if that would help, but pain took over once more, and the images were mixed up again. All she could see was pain.

She looked down at her lap, willing her brain to focus, ignoring the pain. Things started clicking into place. She remembered wearing a fantastic bracelet, and she remembered an old guy staring at it. When? Where? She knew she was with Clark, but the rest was still fuzzy. She looked at the policeman more closely, and a thought popped into her brain. "Are you Gustav? Were you at the restaurant?"

Hearing her say his name caused him to turn back around and walk toward her. "You shouldn't know my name. How do you know that?" He came closer to her face. The menacing look in his eyes made her shudder. "Who are you? What do you know? Who else knows my name?"

This was disturbing to him. Now, he couldn't let the woman live. First, though, he needed her tell him where the jewelry was hidden. He pulled his handgun out of his pocket.

# $\mathcal{N}$inety-Six

ONBOARD THE USS Potomac, Karla had talked to the captain. He was cutting the cruise short and they were headed back to the dock. Clark had been pacing. By now, he had sent four texts and none had been answered.

He placed a call to Roger. "Something's wrong. He's got Marta, but we still don't know where. I won't be able to make it into The City for another hour. It's getting to me just waiting here doing nothing. Will you go check the house? Maybe he left some clue. Maybe she left some clue. I'm just hoping she's still alive."

"Hang in there. I'll head that way right now and drive my car so it doesn't look like the police are involved, in case he's still at the house and watching. I'll keep you posted."

"Thanks. I don't have a good feeling about any of this. Let me know what you find. What's been going down on your end?"

Roger filled him in on all the details as he drove. "We're so close. We've got a whole bunch of the diamonds and other jewelry, plus several passports, and piles of money. He's taken some of the diamonds and stones out of their settings, but it's still all here. We'll know what we're missing after they finish cataloging it. There are some rings, but the piece we're still missing is the ring with the most valuable diamond in it. No sign of that.

"He left no prints in the condo. Wiped clean. But, we did get an address in Puerto Rico where the boxes were supposed to be sent. We're sending a team there. Hopefully, it belongs to Gustav or an accomplice.

"My guys are going into the hotel room at the Ritz as we speak. I'll have more info on that shortly. I can't believe either Mr. Kim or The Ghost is still there, but it's worth a shot. Surveillance hasn't seen anyone leave that floor all day, and we've been watching since 4 a.m.

"What we don't have are Mr. Kim and Gustav. That's disturbing, especially since Gustav has Marta. Any communication from him since this morning?"

"None." Clark sighed. His stomach turned at the thought of her being with that man.

"I'll be at the house in about 15 minutes. There's a bunch of construction, and we've got several streets blocked. Let me know when you're close. Talk to you later."

Clark sat down, put his hands in his head, and tried to think. His phone buzzed with an incoming text.

"Where is the bracelet? I'm becoming frustrated with your girlfriend. She's not talking. I'm giving her two more minutes and then she's done for. If you want to see her alive, tell me where the bracelet and ring are. If you don't, you'll have a mess on your hands."

Abruptly, Clark stood up and almost knocked over Karla. "What's going on?"

"Look at this text. Do you think he's at the house?"

"Yeah, I do. Is Roger headed there?"

"Yeah, but it's going to take a lot longer than two minutes for him to get there. I'm going to answer him and tell him they're in the safe at the house. I'll give him a fake combination. Maybe that will buy enough time, if he's there."

"Do you think that's wise? What if he gets upset when he can't open it?"

"I don't have a lot of choices. Here goes."

Clark sent a text, just telling him they were in the safe.

Immediately, Gustav sent a text. "Where? Don't screw with me or she's history."

Clark sent the location of the safe and a bogus combination, hoping to stall for a little time. Marta's life depended on him. He had never felt so helpless and so frustrated.

The USS Potomac docked, and Clark and Karla rushed off. "I'll meet you there."

# Ninety-Seven

**ROGER'S TEAM OF** agents at the Ritz had just entered the penthouse suite. Two remained outside the suite in the hallway.

What they encountered surprised them.

Sitting in a chair, facing the bank of windows was an old man. Slowly, he swiveled the chair toward them as they came further into the room, weapons drawn. He appeared to be barely alive. His breathing was shallow, his hands were trembling, and eyes were sunken in to his head. Blue veins bulged in his forehead. In his hand was a small handgun, resting in his lap.

One of the agents motioned to the others as he lowered his weapon. "Sir, give me the gun."

The old man mumbled something in Chinese, then in French, then looked at the agent. "My time has come. I do not have my family's bracelet. The old Frenchman stole it from my father, and I cannot clear his honor without getting it back." He lifted the handgun.

Two agents pointed their weapons at him. "Sir. Please give me your gun." They took a small step toward the old man.

"No. It will end here. My son has gone to take care of the thief. I must honor my father. Without the bracelet, I must not live." Hands shaking, he lifted the small handgun to his heart and pulled the trigger. His body jerked as the shot created a muffled sound. His pristine, white shirt slowly turned crimson. It happened so quickly, the agents did not have time to react.

One agent rushed to him, trying to stop the blood flow. Another agent called for an ambulance.

Two other agents searched the suite. The lead agent called Roger to report what had just happened.

"Okay. Secure the scene, take prints, and let me know how the old man is."

One agent shook his head.

"I think he's gone. He was pretty frail. Just thought you should know what he said. He was probably talking about his son going after Gustav. Let me know what else you need. We'll be here."

"Thanks. Later."

# Ninety-Eight

GUSTAV HAD HAD it with Marta. Time was moving too fast. And, he had nothing.

He paced in front of her, mumbling to no one in particular. Marta watched.

Slowly, the pieces were falling into place as her head cleared. Jewelry and Clark. She was sure he wanted the jewelry Clark had been investigating. She still didn't understand why he thought she had it, though. How was she going to convince him she didn't have it? Just as she was trying to think things through, Gustav pulled out his phone and smiled.

"Your boyfriend finally came through. Show me where the safe is."

Puzzled, Marta wasn't sure what he meant. How did Clark know what was going on? Why did Clark tell him about the safe? There were no diamonds in the safe. Where was Clark? She thought he was with everyone else at Gustav's condo. She was so confused.

"I'm losing patience again." He walked toward her, his hand in the air, ready to strike her again. "The safe. Where is it?"

"It's behind the large painting. The one in the den. You need to remove two brackets and then turn the hinges to move the painting."

Gustav looked toward the den. "If you and your boyfriend are messing with me, I'll leave him a big mess to clean up. This better be right." He walked out of her office and toward the den. Shadow came out from behind the desk.

"Shadow, don't." Marta whispered to him, afraid what Gustav would do if he saw him. This was one time she wished for a dog. A big, mean, angry dog.

Several minutes later, Gustav stalked back into her office. "What's going on? The combination he gave me doesn't work. What's the combination?" He stood over her, his gun pointed at her head. Shadow had gone back behind the desk.

Marta had no choice but to give him the real combination. She knew she was dead either way. "It's complicated. You might want to write it down."

He sneered at her as she gave him the numbers. He went back to the safe, and she heard him mumble and then shout.

"Damn it. There's no diamonds in here. Where the hell are my diamonds?" Angrily, he walked back to face Marta. "I am done with you and your games. You've had your chances. You're finished."

He raised his gun to her head, ready to pull the trigger.

# Ninety-Nine

MR. KIM FIGURED he had waited long enough. Several scenarios played out in his mind. The one he kept coming back to was that the policeman who had entered the house was not really a policeman.

"My informants don't screw up. That is Gustav's car. Therefore, that had to be Gustav, disguised as a policeman. But, what is he doing in her house for this long? Is she in this with him? But, if so, why aren't they leaving with the diamonds?

"Something isn't right. I need to go in."

Carefully, he made his way to the front door, weapon drawn. Turning the doorknob, he was pleased to see it wasn't locked. Silently, he pushed open the door.

Stepping softly inside, he could hear Gustav shouting at someone. He walked toward the shouting, careful not to make any noise. Through the doorway to another room he could see the woman tied to a chair, Gustav facing her with his gun pointed at her head.

Gustav yelled. "One last time." He raised his weapon, aimed it at her head, and prepared to fire.

Out behind the desk came a menacing, feral growl as 15 pounds of fur flew at Gustav's thigh, surprising him, and knocking him off balance. Gustav fired but his shot went wild, hitting the ceiling. He screamed as sharp claws connected through the fabric. Shadow darted behind Marta's chair.

Turning around to see where the cat went, he saw a man standing in the doorway, and aimed his weapon at him. Mr. Kim had already assessed the situation and shot Gustav in the chest before he could fire. Gustav went down, blood everywhere. Calmly, Mr. Kim walked up to Gustav as he lay on the polished wood floor, and put two bullets into his head.

As he then turned toward Marta, the same irate cat came charging out from under the chair a second time, taking a swipe at his leg as he ran past, growling. Mr. Kim turned and aimed at Shadow as he scurried around the corner, claws scratching on the wooden floor. A shot rang out.

Mr. Kim looked at Marta, his mouth open, eyes questioning. She was paralyzed by all the action and noise. Concern for Shadow registered foremost in her brain.

Roger stood in the doorway, his weapon in his hand. He watched as Mr. Kim collapsed to the floor in his own pool of blood. Checking to make sure he was no longer a danger, he kicked his weapon away from him, and walked toward Marta.

"I won't ask if you're okay. You need a doctor and probably some stitches from the looks of your face and head." He untied her, as she tried to stand up.

She started to say something. "Shadow . . ." Then, she fainted.

# One Hundred

**ROGER CAUGHT HER** before she hit the floor, laid her on the small sofa, and stood up. Shadow came out, looked at Roger, and hopped up by Marta's head. Roger gave him a quick pet before he stood up to assess what he surmised happened just before he got there.

Not expecting to find a pulse on either man, he double-checked anyway. He had already placed a call for an ambulance and now called for the Medical Examiner as well. Then, he called Clark. "She's okay. She'll need some stitches, but everything is under control." Clark relayed that he and Karla were about 10 minutes away.

He called Ian to let them know what had happened. "Marta can probably fill in the details when she's coherent. She's got a nasty wound on her head, and he must have hit her on the cheek as well. She'll need stitches." He had returned to Marta, motioning for her to stay where she was, as she slowly came to, blinking in confusion. Shadow was sniffing her head as she tried to sit up. He sat down beside her as he continued to talk to Ian.

"Gustav must have been here to find the diamond bracelet he saw her wearing at the restaurant. Not sure why else he would have tied her up and beat her. Mr. Kim must have followed him or he could have been watching the house all along. At any rate,

240

they're both dead. I've got an ambulance coming for Marta. I'm not sure what else my team found at the Ritz. I know I have messages from them."

"I can tell you about that." Ian filled Roger in on the rest of what had happened there. "At this point, we can only assume The Ghost and Mr. Kim were on a mission to get the bracelet, the diamonds, or all of it. We might never know. Then again, we might find out more after The Ghost's mansion here in Paris is completely searched. Take care of Marta and finalize everything there on your end. We'll all meet and talk in a couple of days. Keep me posted if anything new pops up."

"I would venture a guess that we have all the diamonds recovered. We'll know more once my team gets all the boxes to the lab for verification." Roger looked up from his call as Clark and Karla entered the house. "Clark is here. We'll talk to you a little later."

Clark had rushed to Marta's side. She had completely regained consciousness, but was still dazed. Shadow was sitting on her lap. "Oh My God. I thought I had lost you. Again. He sent me a text of you tied up and told me he was going to kill you if I didn't tell him where the bracelet was. I tried to stall for time and gave him a bogus combination to the safe."

Marta smiled at him. "I know. I had to give him the right one. But, he was ready to kill me when he didn't find the bracelet in it." She started to say more, but the EMTs interrupted her.

"Miss, we need to take you to the hospital to be looked over and for stitches." Shadow wouldn't budge. "Can you move the cat?"

Clark picked up Shadow, who reluctantly left Marta's side. The EMTs moved her to the stretcher and then carried her to the waiting ambulance.

Clark motioned to Roger. "I'm going to the hospital with Marta. I'll call when she's taken care of and you can fill me in." He handed Shadow to Roger. Both cat and agent looked surprised.

# Epilogue

**TWO WEEKS LATER,** the task force was meeting for the final time at Clark and Marta's home. Ian had flown in from Paris. Earlier in the day, they had all gathered for a memorial service for Sami. Her funeral had been a private affair, and this was more of a celebration of her life. Models and photographers from all over the world came to show their love for her and their sadness at her life-ending tragedy.

Everyone had grieved and celebrated. Now, they had gone, and the task force was waiting for Ian to bring them up to speed on everything, bringing closure to the case.

Marta's headaches had almost disappeared and the bruises on her face were fading. She sat on the sofa next to Clark, Shadow on her lap. Everyone was still talking about the models and photographers they had met that day.

Ian cleared his throat and raised his glass of wine. "Here's to Marta's recovery, here's to Sami's life, and here's to the final pieces of this bizarre case." Everyone raised their glasses as Shadow jumped down and left the living room.

"I'll wrap up everything I have, and then Roger can fill us in on what he has. Some of this you may already know.

"We've finished processing the mansion outside of Paris. This belonged to the man we had been calling The Ghost, whose real

242

name was John Pierre Kim. His family had a history with Matilda's family, involving gambling, swindling, and possibly murder. We found evidence that their great-grandfathers did indeed have some type of bet or business dealings that involved the one bracelet. The one Sami wore to the party and then sent to Karla, the one Marta wore to the restaurant. Mr. Kim and his father were at that restaurant, but we don't believe they saw the bracelet at that time.

"His mansion has provided us with closure to many jewel heists over the last several decades. There's more, but at this point it's not relevant to this case. Mary Wong was the one who provided the address and for that, we will be eternally grateful to her. It's just terrible she had to die because of her involvement." He raised his glass in a toast to Mary and then continued.

"When Gustav contacted Mr. Kim about the jewelry he had for sale, he must have mentioned the bracelet. Or, Mr. Kim knew about the heist, and was hoping this was THE bracelet. We really don't know how that transaction first took place. I guess Mr. Kim could have been watching Matilda's place, too. At this point, it doesn't matter.

"Both Mr. Kim and Gustav were wanted by Interpol, for various crimes. We aren't sure if they had had dealings with each other before this one or not." He paused, looked around the room, and continued.

"Roger, what did your guys find at their hotel room?"

"For one thing, the room had been wiped of prints. They had the sheets and towels in a box, packed suitcases, and ready to leave. We were able to grab their plane and pilots, who were basically employees. They didn't really know much about their business. We did learn a lot from their flight plans, and where they had been. We assume Mr. Kim was going to get the bracelet from either Gustav or Marta, head to the airport, and both of them were leaving together.

"Although, the old man was really frail. He could hardly hold the gun before he shot himself.

"We also recovered the rest of the diamonds and jewelry from the boxes Gustav had given to the night manager to send for him. It was our good fortune he was late for class and didn't have time to mail them. They have all been catalogued and accounted for, with the exception of the large ring.

"Our agents have been to the address in Puerto Rico, which was where Gustav was sending them. We've recovered more jewels there, his computers, access to his bank accounts, weapons, disguises, and money. He had quite the operation going.

"And, get this. Just like here, his neighbors all described him differently. He truly was a master of disguises."

Clark had gotten up and refilled everyone's glasses. Shadow had come back into the room, and was playing with a toy mouse under the chair.

Ian thanked everyone for their part in solving each piece of this puzzle as his phone buzzed and he excused himself.

Marta spoke up. "I want to thank everybody for getting to me as quickly as you did. I believe Gustav was ready to kill me. The look on his face when he discovered the safe didn't have his bracelet or other diamonds was the scariest look I have ever seen. When he raised his gun to my head, I can't begin to describe how terrified I was. I knew it was over. And, I didn't want him to hurt Shadow." She bent down to pet Shadow, who meowed. She threw his mouse down the hall and he chased after it.

Roger nodded to her. "From what you've said, Shadow played an important part in Gustav's aim being off."

"Yeah. I think his loud growl surprised him and then alarmed him, which briefly took his focus off me. Then, his claws must have done enough damage to Gustav's leg for him to be distracted. I suppose that's how Mr. Kim was able to shoot him so quickly. I never heard or saw him come in."

Roger nodded and stood up. "Good to know that cat looks out for you. I'm not planning on crossing him." He also gave Shadow a quick back rub as Shadow darted behind a chair, chasing his mouse or his imaginary friends.

Ian had returned. "One last piece of news. Our lab confirms what Roger said. We have every single piece from Matilda's collection in Paris. Except for one thing. The most valuable, spectacular ring. We never found it anywhere. Best guess, it's at the bottom of the Pacific. Her foundation is elated to have it all back and wants to thank us all personally. If you ever get to Paris, be sure to let them know. They would love to meet each one of you."

Karla nodded. "I was just thinking about the ring. Sami must have hidden it in a pocket or in the purse she had with her, and that's what she meant when she told me it was safe. I really think she thought that by keeping it with her, she'd know where it was at all times. That sounds exactly like something she would do. But, it's really a shame." She smiled as Shadow came out from under her chair and rubbed against her leg.

Karla had set the dark blue Prada purse by her chair. Shadow had noticed the logo placard dangling from the end of the purse, and was now batting at it. She looked down at him and smiled again. "Crazy cat of yours, Marta. He loves this little tag on my purse. Guess he has expensive taste." Everyone chuckled.

"Leave it to him to find something and adopt it as his toy. You'd be surprised at the things he steals from my office and chases around the house."

Ian raised his glass in a toast. "Thanks again to all of you. I will need any reports you haven't yet turned in. Otherwise, I'm considering this case closed." Everyone did likewise, and then talked among themselves for a few minutes.

Karla stood up. "Thanks again to all of you for helping me get through this mess with Sami, too. I appreciate it. And, thanks for helping with the memorial for her and the party here. I'm sure she's smiling down on us right now." She looked toward the Heavens, and then reached under the chair for her purse. Shadow had almost completely burrowed his head inside it, and it slid away from her as she reached for it.

"Shadow. Get out of Karla's purse. You don't need to be messing with it. She has nothing in it for cats."

He backed his head out of the purse, batted at something, and went chasing it down the polished hardwood floor into the hallway.

"He probably stole a pen. He loves playing with them. Or, he hid one of his mice in your purse. It's a game to him." Marta shook her head. "If he took a pen, you'll probably never find it again. I have no idea where he stashes the ones he takes from me. I'm sorry, Karla. I don't think he's ever stolen anything out of someone else's purse before, though, so he must like you." Marta looked at Clark who walked down the hall toward Shadow.

"Well, son of a bitch. Guess what he has?" He took the toy away from Shadow and brought it back to the living room. Holding it up for all to see, was a jaw-dropping, diamond ring. Every person gasped as the 15-karat diamond grabbed all the sunlight from the windows, and bounced it around the room. Shadow followed him, chasing the prisms of light as they danced up the walls and back to the floor.

Silence filled the room as everyone stared at what Clark was holding.

"Spectacular doesn't even begin to describe that." Karla was the first to speak as she stared at the ring in Clark's hand.

"When she said it was safe, I guess it really was. In her favorite purse. She probably thought I would look here first and find it. And, I've been carrying this purse for a week. Oh my. What if I would have lost it? Sami, you never cease to amaze me.

"And, thanks to Shadow, we found it. You deserve extra treats for this, big guy."

Shadow meowed as he lunged at another prism of light on the wall.

"Mystery solved, everybody. Thanks to Sami and Shadow, this case really is closed." Ian held his glass toward Shadow in a toast.

# About the Author

**WENDY VANHATTEN IS** a published author, editor-in-chief for "Prime Time Living Magazine," wine, food, and travel editor for "WEMagazine," and travel enthusiast. She has taught writing at the college level, writing workshops, and is affiliated with Bay Area Travel Writer Organization, www.batw.org/.

Her children's books, the *Max and Myron* series, teach children to read while developing good character traits.

Travel advice and photos are updated weekly on her blog at www.travelsandescapes.blogspot.com. Her books are available online at Amazon or from her website, www.wendyvanhatten.com.

# Additional Titles by Wendy VanHatten

My Life, The Sequel: A Girlfriend's Guide to Personal Success

When the Cat Speaks . . . Listen: A purr . . . fectly good way to enjoy life

Dad's Hidden Box

### HIDDEN TRUTHS SERIES

Champagne Lies
Vineyard Secrets
Dark Legacy
The Secret of the Purloined Bracelet
The Forger's Key

### MAX & MYRON SERIES

by Wendy VanHatten and R David Kryder with illustrations by Corie Barloggi

Max and Myron Learn Please and Thank You Max and Myron, My First Day of School
Max and Myron I'm Sorry, Please Forgive Me Max & Myron Learn Please Don't Tease
Max & Myron Learn Big and Small, Short and Tall
The Authorship Journey: A profitable adventure? by Wendy Van-hatten, Ginger Marks, Misty Taggart, and Tracee Gleichner

Available on Amazon.com and fine bookstores everywhere.

www.ingramcontent.com/pod-product-compliance
Lightning Source LLC
Chambersburg PA
CBHW021236250626
47155CB00008B/3039